ECHOES OF THE OTHERWORLD

BOOK ONE OF THE SONGS OF THE CROWMOTHER

by
DONALD QUILL

ISBN 979-8-9989881-0-3

This is a work of fiction. Names, characters, places, and incidents are either the product of the author's imagination or are used fictitiously. Any resemblance to actual persons, living or dead, events, or locales is entirely coincidental.

First Edition

For information or permissions, contact:
donaldquill.author@gmail.com

Published by Forgotten Rites Publishing

FORGOTTEN
RITES
PUBLISHING

An imprint of sacred memory

To The Morrígan,
She who watches from the veil,
Who speaks in crow-feather and flame,
Who remembers what the world forgets.
This tale is for You,
Whisperer of omens, keeper of the oath,
Lady of shadow and sovereignty.
May every word serve as offering.
May every silence carry Your name.
— Your flame-born scribe,
D.Q.

They came in ships, and in flame, and in wind, and the land
remembered their names."
— *Lebor Gabála Érenn*
(*mythic account of the Tuatha Dé Danann*)

Historical & Cultural Note

Echoes of the Otherworld is a work of historical fantasy rooted in the mythic landscape of 1st-century Ireland. While the story is fictional, its spiritual, linguistic, and cultural foundations are drawn from early Celtic cosmology, Iron Age ritual practice, and surviving Irish mythological cycles, particularly those surrounding Brú na Bóinne, The Morrígan, and the Tuatha Dé Danann.

Rituals, festivals (such as Samhain), and sacred sites (including Uaimh na gCat and Tara) are depicted with care to align with archaeological records, reconstructed oral traditions, and early poetic texts. The role of druids as spiritual memory-keepers, the significance of ancestral communion, and the sovereign presence of female deities reflect the fluid and deeply symbolic worldview of ancient Gaelic societies.

While creative liberties have been taken in dialogue and structure, every effort has been made to ensure the mythic integrity and cultural reverence of the world portrayed.

PROLOGUE

BENEATH THE HEARTHSTONE

Before the stones forgot, before the crows fell silent,

there was a flame that memory could not drown.

She bore no crown, yet the world bowed, or burned.

Long before the flames whispered her name, Ríona lived by the river's bend, where trees bowed in sacred hush and stones remembered songs older than speech. Dragonflies flickered like fire spirits among the reeds, and the wind braided whispers of forgotten rites. She was not yet vessel nor chosen, only a girl with ash-smudged fingers, a wreath of elder bark in her hair, and a hunger for the songs sung beneath her breath.

***

The hearth still crackled in the dim light, its smoke braided with the scent of peat, wild garlic, and goat's milk warmed over stone. Woven mats of rushes softened the cold clay beneath her bare feet. A bone-handled knife rested near a bowl of crushed hazelnuts, waiting for morning meal preparations. Beyond the woven doorway, a low bleat echoed, one of the spring lambs, born too early.

She believed the land spoke if one only listened closely enough. That every flick of cattail or twist of root bore the imprint of something old, something watching. Even then, she felt the world move differently around her, as though the river paused to hear her thoughts, and the crows that circled above did not simply watch but remembered.

She would wander the glade barefoot, whispering songs she half-invented, half-remembered, her voice barely louder than the rustling reeds. The air carried her words like offerings. Sometimes, she would find small gifts on her path, an uncracked acorn, a feather shaped like a crescent moon, a stone with a spiral carved faintly into its belly. She called these the land's answers.

***

Her mother, Ainé, the village herb-wife, walked between worlds with silence and sharp laughter. She wore her hair coiled and tied with crow feathers, and her robes bore the scent of mugwort, yarrow, and the ashes of solstice fires. She taught Ríona the fire's tongue, how to braid rushes for Brigid's Day, and how to set offerings of bread and berries on the altar of stones where moonlight knelt. In her gaze burned the knowing, a flame fed by ancestry and oath, ritual and root.

Her mother had sung healing songs for the sick.
Her grandmother had read omens in crow feathers and river foam. The priestess line had not broken, it had only softened, whispered forward. Ríona was the breath that carried it on.

"Watch the smoke," her mother would say, lifting a bowl over the hearth. "If it leans to the left, The Morrígan walks nearby. If it vanishes straight, she waits behind the veil."

Ríona remembered those words. And others too, from seasons long passed. Imbolc fires crackling behind lambing pens.

Brigid's crosses damp with dew. The sickle songs of Lughnasadh, when the grain bent beneath calloused hands and

2

every breath felt borrowed from the sun. The wheel had always turned. But now it buckled.

***

They sat cross-legged by the hearth, their fingers busy with roots and thread, weaving nettle cord and tale alike. Her mother guided her hand when she fumbled the braiding pattern, murmuring, "No rush, flame-heart. Even The Morrígan waits for a knot well-tied." Ríona would giggle, her brow furrowed with concentration as she worked the cord, and her mother would tap her gently on the shoulder with a sprig of yarrow when she got it right.

"Now tell the cord a secret," her mother instructed one evening. "A wish, a vow, or a truth you dare not say aloud."

Ríona paused, unsure. "What if the cord forgets?"

"It won't. But you might," her mother said. "So let it hold your memory until you're strong enough to carry it again."

On stormy nights, her mother taught her to listen to the wind for names. They'd sit at the threshold, a bowl of salt on one side and a feather on the other.

"Why the salt?" Ríona had asked.

"To ground you. The wind can carry more than whispers if you're not careful."

"And the feather?"

"That's for flight. You'll understand when you need to."

Ríona once asked if her father had also heard the wind.

Her mother's hands were stilled. "He heard it once. But he turned away from it. That's why I taught you to listen longer."

After the stories ended, Ríona sometimes would whisper: "Will I walk between the worlds like you?"

And her mother would answer without turning: "No, my flame-daughter. You will walk where even I cannot follow."

It frightened her, sometimes, this promise of separation. What if the path she walked erased the very roots that made her? What if the songs she learned in shadow drowned out her own voice?

3

One dusk, beneath a Samhain sky, streaked with burnt orange and the cries of migrating geese, her mother stood beside her in the doorway longer than usual. Her hands lingered at Ríona's shoulders as she braided a lock of her hair.

"There are paths in this world that circle back and others that vanish behind you the moment you step onto them," she said softly.

Ríona looked up. "Which path is mine?"

Her mother didn't answer immediately. Her gaze traced the horizon, the shifting clouds, the way the trees leaned toward the wind. "You'll walk the kind that asks for more than it gives. I've watched the signs for years, and they all say the same thing: you are not meant to stay hidden in this valley. But I wish you were."

She crouched and placed her hands over Ríona's. "If you ever forget who you are, find the nettles. They'll sting, but they'll remember. They always remember."

Then, with a breath that felt too heavy for the moment, she took her daughter's hand.

She led her into the bone-ring of elder trees. The grove was a temple untouched by the blade, where the air hummed with reverence. In its center stood a stone, flat, quartz-laced, carved with ancient spirals that pulsed faintly under twilight. Offerings of crow feathers, worn coins, and tiny dolls of cornhusk circled its base.

"Place your hand on it," her mother said, voice low as prayer. "Not with thought. With breath."

Ríona obeyed. The stone's chill kissed her skin, then warmed with a living thrum. Around them, the world held its breath. No bird sang. No leaves moved. Her heartbeat rose like the echo of drums in a burial mound.

The silence stretched, thick as fog, brittle as frost. Even the reeds seemed to hold their breath. Something unseen trembled just beyond the veil of sight, as if the land itself waited for a name to be spoken.

Then it came.

Not a voice. A presence.

A crow, cloaked in ember and ash, stood in her vision upon a battlefield strewn with oath-bound dead. Its eyes, dark as sacred wells, burned with knowing. Around its talons lay the relics of fallen warriors, shields broken in sacrifice, blades rusted from mourning. They sang of forgotten names and undone rites.

The air thickened with scent: blood-warm iron, burning heather, crushed juniper, and the sweet decay of lavender left too long on a shrine. Distant thunder rolled like the breath of an old god, and the canopy above trembled without wind.

She flinched. Pulled back. Her mother watched in silence, her nod a gesture older than language.

"Some are born to hear what the world has buried," she whispered. "And some to become its voice."

That night, Ríona dreamed of a river flowing in reverse, its water aglow with memory. A woman stood beneath the moon, cloaked in feathers and crowned with antlers. Her arms were outstretched in benediction, her voice a flame that spoke in silence. From her lips came a lullaby in the tongue of flame and bone.

A single feather, black streaked with ember-red, rested on her pillow at dawn. Its shaft throbbed gently with warmth as though remembering flight.

She wrapped it in a rushes cloth and tucked it into a box lined with thyme and protective knotwork.

But before she sealed it, she held it in her hands and whispered, just loud enough for the fire to catch:

"Let me remember who I am, even if the world forgets."

What lingered most was not the fire's heat but its sacred hush. Her mother moved with reverence, even in silence. Her words lowered when she named the old gods. The way she once said,

"You will walk paths I never will, flame-daughter. But let the scent of nettles remind you where you began."

At night, before dreams turned to visions, Ríona lay beneath the creaking birch, listening to the fire's pulse and the spirits shifting beyond the veil. Shadows lengthened along the thatch, curling toward her like tendrils from the Otherworld, and she welcomed them.

But sometimes, as the wind curled beneath the thatch and the fire dimmed low, she wondered:

What if I am shaped into something the world needs but not something I remember? What if I trade memory for myth?

The world was never quiet then. It was full, a song of leaf and flame, memory and myth.

And in that fullness, her first silence was born.

ACT I

The Thread Unraveled

Before the path is chosen, the breath must break.

Before the name is spoken, it must be forgotten.

CHAPTER 1

THE RED VEIL

In the hush beneath the elder boughs,

a name was given, not by breath, but by stone, river, and crow.

A name meant to endure even when the gods were forgotten.

T he early light filtered through the mist that clung to the ancient stones of Brugh na Bóinne. The land stirred with life, still caught in the hush of dawn, but Ríona had already begun her morning ritual. Her ember-red hair spilled down her back in loose braids, catching the mistlight like a living flame. Pale as bone ash, her skin bore the faint blue ink of old rites, and her eyes—dark hazel flecked with gold—held the stillness of riverstone, ever watching, ever remembering. Smoke rose from the altar in delicate coils, carrying the scent of yarrow and pine. Her voice, low and melodic, wove through the fog like a thread through cloth.

The offerings were humble, bread, milk, crushed berries, but they carried the weight of generations. She placed them one by one before the goddess's stone, carved with spiral knots and crow feathers pinned with ash twine. These were not just tokens; they were promises and covenants. Ríona knelt, pressing her palms into the earth.

"May your silence carry truth. May your shadow mark the path," she whispered, words meant for the Morrigan alone.

***

A wind rose suddenly, cold and smelling of iron. The smoke scattered. Her breath caught. Something stirred beyond the trees.

When she stood, the feeling lingered, not fear, something older, expectation. Her gaze drifted to the eastern ridge, where sunrise bled faint color into the clouds. The air shimmered briefly above the altar, and for a breathless moment, she saw a crow-shaped blur in the light. Then it was gone.

***

She walked the path back toward the village with her thoughts wrapped tight. A hush seemed to follow her as she passed between Hazel and Elder. Even the birds withheld their song. Ríona paused to touch the bark of an oak whose roots curled like knotted limbs over the trail.

"What are you trying to tell me?" she murmured.

The oak gave no answer.

She veered off the main trail and climbed toward the high ridge that overlooked the western hills. At its crest stood a worn stone pillar draped in ivy, a boundary marker older than the village itself. Ríona knelt before it and opened a pouch at her belt, removing a vial of sacred ash and a bundle of dried rowan twigs. She anointed the stone and scattered the twigs to the wind.

"Let no unclean step pass without reckoning. Let no shadow cross this land without notice," she intoned.

She pressed a blackthorn pin into the soil beside the stone and whispered an ancient word. It was a rite of protection, not done lightly, not since the last flood had brought sickness to the cattle three winters ago. But the feeling in her chest would not ease.

The wind caught her cloak as she stood. Somewhere below, a distant dog barked once and fell silent.

10

Her work was done. Yet the silence that followed felt like a held breath.

***

The village of Brúgh breathed softly in the morning fog. Thatched roofs shimmered with dew, and smoke whispered from hearth vents. A child chased a goat through the damp straw, laughing until he saw Ríona and stopped abruptly. He bowed awkwardly.

She smiled gently. "Mind the stones when you run. They remember who falls."

"Yes, High Priestess," he stammered, grabbing the goat's collar.

She passed the stone wall that marked the village's heart. Two elders sat on benches beneath the willow, plucking herbs and murmuring about omens. They fell silent as she approached, offering brief nods.

Inside the healing hut, she checked dried roots and tightened braids of wild garlic hung over the lintel. Ainé's voice echoed in memory: "Every hearth is a temple. Keep it prepared."

The Circle held many titles—Priestess, Druid, Archdruid, Keeper of Flame, Seer of Stone—but none without cost. Priestesses like Ríona bore the memory of the land, walking as bridges between past and present, voice and silence. Archdruids carried prophecy, often aging too quickly under the weight of visions that stole sleep and joy alike. Druids guarded the chants, the rites, the thresholds between worlds, giving up family, names, and even time to do so.

But power was never freely given. Each ritual, each invocation, exacted its price—an offering not of coin, but of breath, blood, or memory. Some left their voices behind to walk deeper into trance. Others surrendered years of life for one moment of clarity in sacred flame. There were songs that could blind the singer to the waking world, chants that echoed so loud within the soul they left no room for dreams.

Even the lesser rites left marks—hair streaked with ash-gray, dreams soaked in salt, fingers twitching in rhythm with chants long since ended. These were not stories. They were truths. Known, accepted, endured. For the land did not give power to those unwilling to be changed.

She opened the herbal ledger. The ink was fading, but she still remembered every line. Her hand hovered over the page, then she stilled. Something deeper than habit held her still, an intuition pressing into her bones.

Footsteps sounded outside. A figure waited beyond the curtain of beads.

"Enter," she said.

A young druid-in-training, Fira, stepped inside. Her robes were clean, her eyes wide—but not with innocence. There was something taut in her posture, as if she carried more than the message she'd been told to deliver.

"Archdruid Fareth has called a gathering. All Circle members are to attend."

Ríona looked up. "What is it?"

Fira hesitated. "He didn't say. Only that it concerns the prophecy."

She shifted, glancing toward the hearth before speaking again. "The elders will not like it. To speak of the prophecy beyond the tuath is to risk breaking the Circle's trust. And... some think the prophecy should remain buried."

Ríona studied her. "And what do you think, Fira?"

A pause. Then, with eyes lowered, Fira answered, "I think you frighten them—because you listen without fear. Some of us... still envy that."

The words hung between them like smoke. Fira adjusted the edge of her sleeve and turned before Ríona could reply.

Fira hesitated. "The elders will not like it. To speak of the prophecy beyond the tuath is to risk breaking the Circle's trust, and the chieftain's silence holds weight in matters such as these."

Ríona didn't flinch. "Then let him speak it aloud. Until he does, I will not be bound by fear disguised as custom."

Before leaving, Ríona added an offering to her mother's old shrine in the rear of the hut—nettles woven with red thread and blackthorn. A small silver charm in the shape of a spiral rested there, tarnished with age. She brushed her thumb across its surface.

"Remember," she whispered. "As you did for me, I will for them."

She lingered a moment longer. Memories surfaced like mist, her mother's laughter as they stirred herbs, the firm grip of her hands during the first blood rite, the lullaby sung in a tongue older than fire.

"If I call and you don't answer," she said quietly, "will I still hear you in the crows?"

The silence in the hut pressed close. A nettle leaf brushed her skin. She flinched, not from pain, but from the sudden certainty that her mother was listening.

She let the silence stretch. It pressed in, not empty, but expectant, as if the air itself held its breath. Beneath her fingers, the worn edge of her mother's altar felt warm, as though memory had not yet cooled. Outside, a crow called once, sharp and clear, and the sound seemed to echo through the marrow of the stone.

She did not answer aloud. There was no need. The promise had already woven itself into the red thread, the blackthorn, the bone.

As she turned from the shrine, the faintest breeze stirred the herbs hanging overhead. She paused, breathing in the scent of dried nettle and rue, grounding herself in the old ways, ways that still watched, still waited.

She slipped into her cloak, fastened the crow-feather brooch at her collar, and stepped back into the gray light of morning.

The Circle met within the bone ring, a grove of standing elder trees that formed a perfect circle around a flat stone altar. Their bark was white with age, and their leaves whispered in the windless air. The ground beneath their roots was etched with old blood sigils, nearly faded now but still humming faintly in Ríona's senses.

The wind did not enter the bone ring. It stopped at the edge as if afraid to trespass. Above, a single crow circled once and vanished into a cloud.

Fareth stood at the center, his ash staff planted in moss.

"The signs have returned," he began. "The rivers reverse. Crows gather by the hundreds in daylight. Fires hiss before lighting."

Murmurs broke through the ranks. Ríona remained silent.

"The Heartstone has awakened."

Now, the hush was complete.

Fareth continued. "It calls westward. Toward the aisles. Toward the hollowed places. But the one to retrieve it must be marked."

He turned toward her.

"Ríona of the Red Veil. You are named in the dream."

She said nothing, but her heart pounded like a drum before the storm.

"You would walk beyond the bounds of this tuath without sanction?" one of the druids asked, voice brittle with unspoken fear.

"No omen from the chieftain's seer, no blessing from our hearth-circle. Prophecy does not excuse rebellion, child."

Ríona held his gaze. "And fear does not excuse silence."

That evening, the druids dispersed, but Fareth lingered. He placed a hand on her shoulder as the others filed away.

14

"You need not walk this path alone," he said quietly. "You know the gods speak, but so too do men. Seek your counsel among the living."

She nodded but said nothing. Her path had already narrowed.

The pool reflected nothing now, no stars, no sky. Only shadow and the stillness she carried within. Ríona pressed her palm to the water's surface, and it did not ripple. She wondered if, in the turning of this path, she would leave even her reflection behind.

***

That night, the stars scattered like cold ash over the valley. Ríona sat beside the sacred pool, moonlight caught in the reeds. The water was still, and the air clung close, thick with things unspoken.

Aedric approached from the grove path. The young druid's footsteps were light, but she heard him.

"You should be inside," he said softly.

"And miss the one place the world still listens?" Ríona replied.

He hesitated, then lowered himself beside her.

"They say the prophecy speaks of sacrifice," he said. "That those who go west do not return unchanged."

"Then they are wise to fear," she said, her voice a whisper. "Because the stones already know my name."

He studied her for a long moment as if trying to memorize her before she changed.

***

When he left, the wind rose again. A crow landed on the stone beside her, its feathers slick with night. It did not call. I only watched it.

Ríona closed her eyes. A voice filled her, not spoken, but known.

"You are chosen. Not for what you carry, but for what you must give up."

The words curled through her chest like smoke.

The wind carried the last of the incense away. The trees leaned in.

She whispered into the stillness: "I am ready."

But in truth, she wasn't sure she ever would be.

The land was changing.

And she had already left the world she knew.

CHAPTER 2

The Silence Beneath the Stones

The morning had a heaviness to it.

Ríona felt it in her lungs before her feet touched the stone. Not the heaviness of weather, no storm brewed above Brú na Bóinne. The skies were clear, the air dry. And yet the silence pressed down like sodden wool, clinging to her skin as she stepped into the spiral.

She began her walk.

The path circled inward, seven coils in total. Each one narrower, each step slower. The quartz beneath her bare feet pulsed faintly in the morning light, warm in places where no sun had yet touched. She sang low as she walked, a chant not meant to be heard but to be felt. It resonated in her chest more than her throat.

"From the still stone, rise. From the risen breath, speak. From the spoken name, remember."

Each verse came softer than the last.

This was not a rite for spectacle. It was for attunement for listening.

But nothing answered.

The cairn, usually so alive with breath and presence, felt sealed. The stones gave off no warmth. The inner chamber, where she would kneel to offer the flame oil, remained dark, as if it refused her light.

***

She paused before entering. Her hand hovered over the central altar stone. A soft spiral had been carved there long ago, but today, it felt faint beneath her fingers, as though the stone itself was forgetting.

A breeze passed overhead, but the leaves didn't stir; even the crows, her constant witnesses, were absent.

Ríona exhaled through her nose and placed a drop of oil in the hollow, lighting it with a word only the spirits should know. It flickered, uncertain, before catching. The flame was pale today. Blue white, not gold.

She stepped back.

There was no shift in the air. No presence rising to greet her. No voice murmured through the bone-colored mist of the mound.

It was not refusal.

It was absence. It was not refusal. It was waiting.

A waiting that felt like breath held between worlds. The stones did not reject her,
they simply had not yet spoken.

She did not leave the cairn.

Not immediately.

Ríona sat on the cold stone floor, legs folded beneath her, hands resting on her knees. Her fingers formed the old triad, thumb to middle finger, forefinger raised. She sat on the cold stone floor, legs folded beneath her, hands resting on her knees. The stone's chill seeped through her skin and marrow.

***

Darkness came not like a curtain but like water, slow, cold, inevitable. She let it swallow her gently.

And as the chamber thickened around her, a voice in her own mind whispered:

What if the gods made a mistake?

The thought struck sharp, unbidden. She buried it beneath the old triad gesture, thumb and middle finger clasped, forefinger raised, but it clung.

What if you are only a vessel because no better soul answered?

The cairn's ancestral hum should have reassured her. It did not.

Her breath stilled. She wasn't afraid of death. She feared vanishing into something she couldn't name, of forgetting the small, stubborn girl who once braided nettles and whispered promises to the stones.

She pressed her fingers harder into the altar until the spiral carved beneath her skin hummed faintly in answer.

"Remember me," she mouthed into the dark, though no voice rose to carry it.

A gesture older than the chants. Older than the Circle itself. The stones had taught her this.

She closed her eyes.

***

The world outside narrowed to the chamber's breath, the hum of quartz, the iron scent of soil, her pulse, and then, not her own: another rhythm beneath her heartbeat, the ancestral thrum. She slipped beneath herself as the cairn blurred away.

The stillness deepened, not with peace, but with pressure, a silence so dense it hummed in her bones. Ríona breathed in slowly, tasting copper and stone, letting the cold seat of the cairn press into her skin like a second spine.

Thoughts fell away, shed like a cloak at the doorway between worlds.

She did not drift.

She sank.

Time slowed. The dark thickened. Somewhere behind her ribs, the spiral mark began to pulse, not with pain, but with recognition.

And then,

She stood in a different place now, liminal, fog-wreathed, more echo than the world. The vision did not arrive all at once. It layered itself—first as memory, then as dream, then as something older. Her mother's presence was the first thread, clear and steady, grounding her in the shape of the known. But beyond that familiarity, other voices waited, ancestral and divine, whispering truths not meant for waking minds. This was the hollow between breath and name. She had come here many times, yet it never looked the same.

***

The sky was silver-black, and the ground beneath her was not ground at all but a memory of earth. Shapes formed from mist, stone towers, tree roots, a broken loom.

And then her mother appeared. Not walking. Not summoned. Just there.

She wore the same robe she had died in, deep moss green, embroidered with the sigil of the first matron-priestess. Her face was clear, not aged or decayed. Her eyes, dark and steady, looked right into her.

"Ríona," she said, though her lips did not move. "You walk too close."

Ríona swallowed. "The cairn was empty. The flame spoke nothing."

"It cannot speak what has been forgotten."

"By whom?" Ríona stepped to the edge of the stream, but did not follow. The water moved against time itself, its backward flow catching the moonlight in pale ribbons that shimmered like breath. She felt no cold, only the weight of knowing.

A scent rose from the stream, lavender singed by fire, elderflower damp with frost. It clung to her skin like a memory unclaimed. The stars above pulsed slower than they should, dimming one by one as if forgetting how to shine.

The Silent Warrior shifted — barely. A measured movement, just enough to draw her awareness back to the present.

He stepped beside her, silent as bone, and positioned himself between her and the cairn's dark mouth. One hand hovered loosely at his side — not reaching for a weapon, not offering comfort, simply *there*.

He did not speak. He never did. But in that moment, his presence felt like a promise: *You do not fall alone.*

A sudden shift. Her breath caught, and something sharp slid beneath her heel — a shard of bone or glass? She crouched, brushing the soil. Nothing. But the wind had changed. The trees no longer hummed; they listened.

She wanted to speak, to ask what waited beyond the water, but the question held no shape. Words felt brittle here, too fragile to carry meaning. So instead, she stood still, hoping the grove, or her mother, would remember what she could not.

The grove hushed around her, not in silence, but in reverence, as if the hollow itself remembered something sacred just out of reach.

The wind curled low around her ankles, no longer chilled, but listening. Somewhere beneath the moss, the earth exhaled, not breath, but memory.

Her mother turned away. She knelt beside a stream that had not been there before, running backward through a bed of blackened reeds.

"When names are no longer spoken in ritual," she said, dipping her fingers into the current, "they become unstable. They return to the earth and wait to be reborn. But if too many vanish too quickly..."

The water turned to ash between her fingers.

Ríona stepped forward. "Is that what's happening? Are we forgetting too fast?"

Her mother didn't answer. Instead, she looked up at the sky. Something enormous stirred behind the clouds, a shadow in the shape of wings.

"The Thread is thinning," she said. "The veil is not the only thing that kept us apart. The gods feared what would happen if mortals remembered everything too quickly."

"What do I do?"

"You listen," she said. "Not for answers. For fractures. For absences."

Before Ríona could respond, her mother's form began to unravel. The wind took her first, and then her outline dissolved into mist. The moss robe remained folded where she had stood.

And then the voice changed. A thousand whispers filled the air, spirits not yet reborn, ancestors too restless to rest. Most passed over her like a breeze, but one lingered, hovered near. A small voice, trembling, familiar: "She left her name under the stone." Ríona tried to reach for it, but it fled.

The whispers faded. Silence stretched, dense and waiting. Ríona bent, brushing the moss robe her mother left behind. It was still warm. She folded it without speaking.

Above, the sky churned. That winged shape circled still, unseen but near.

Where water once flowed, only ash remained.

Breasal's voice came faint behind her. "She carried the old names."

Ríona knelt at the dry streambed. Her fingers touched stone, spiraled, worn.

The spiral pulsed once.

The voice returned:

"She left her name under the stone."

Ríona bowed her head.

"Then I will carry it," she said, "even if I forget my own."

And the vision collapsed.

***

She woke in the cairn, breath shallow, eyes wet. The altar stone had dimmed. Even the pale flame was gone.

She was not alone in the chamber, but whatever had remained... had not stayed. That night, Ríona did not seek sleep, it found her.

She lay on her stone pallet, arms crossed over her chest, her breath slowed by ritual tea, yarrow and valerian laced with elderflower ash. The dormitory air was still. Others had already succumbed to sleep, their dreams no doubt quiet.

But Ríona's were not.

The moment her eyes closed; she fell inward.

Darkness.

Not void, but weighted black, like peat soaked in sorrow. She stood barefoot on scorched ground that hissed faintly with each step. Above her, the sky was wrong. Stars pulsed like open wounds. A ringed moon bled light in ribbons.

She was not alone.

Crows circled above in tight spirals, moving too fast for wings. Their cries were not cries but riddles torn into the air.

"When the earth forgets your name, speak the one beneath the stone."

"When flame does not burn, beware the shadow that does."

"A vow sleeps in your marrow. But whose?"

The wind pulled at her hair, though there was no wind. It whispered through her bones, threading fragments of forgotten songs into the spaces between heartbeats. Each note carried weight, as though it had been buried long and was now clawing its way back.

She turned slowly, searching the horizon for the source, but there was no edge, no sky, no boundary. Only the endless darkness of memory made manifest, and the faint echo of her own breath, reminding her that she still lived, even here.

In the center of the scorched field lay a stone, not gray, but veined with amber. Cracked down the center, it pulsed with inner light.

Ríona stepped forward, drawn by it.

As she approached, her hands began to warm and then burn. Her fingertips glowed, first dull red, then brilliant gold, as the fire beneath her skin awakened. She fell to her knees, hands outstretched over the stone.

And it answered...

CHAPTER 3

WHISPERS BEYOND THE MIST

T he wind had changed. It was not just a shift in current but something older, like a forgotten breath exhaling from the earth. It swept through Brú na Bóinne like a warning, rustling the reedbeds along the Boyne and stirring the ash from long-dead ceremonial fires. It carried scents that didn't belong to the morning: crushed juniper, hot stone, and something sharper, like blood spilled on ancient soil.

***

Ríona stood at the upper cairn's edge, its white quartz stones gleaming faintly from the pre-dawn mist. She wasn't alone, but she felt as if she were the last figure etched into the land before the gods turned their faces away.

The land, usually humming with hidden voices, had gone still.

No birds sang.

Even the sheep in the distant pastures stood motionless, heads tilted toward the west.

She drew her cloak tighter, not against cold, but against the strange stillness pressing against her ribs. A hollow, humming thing, like the silence before a bell tolls. Her fingers traced the spiral tattoo etched down her left arm, not out of habit but for grounding.

In that stillness, a memory rose like a scent.

She had seen this sky before.

***

In a dream years ago. A child's vision that had never left her. A sky stretched too thin. A crow that bled gold from its eyes. And a stone, not dead but alive, cracked open to reveal fire at its core.

They told her that it was just imagination. That the gods had spoken in metaphor.

But she remembered. And the moment she saw the sky that morning, she knew the time had come.

***

That was when the footsteps arrived behind her, slow and deliberate.

"You've been summoned," said a voice she knew well.

It was Naeva, cloaked in a raven feather shawl and mist. Her tone was brittle.

"The Archdruid waits in the Circle of Judgment."

"You've been summoned," said Naeva, her raven-feather shawl brushing the mist.

Ríona did not turn immediately. She stared westward, where the sky bled thin, and the stones whispered no songs.

"I knew he would," she said at last, though the words tasted hollow.

Behind her steady voice, the old fear stirred again,

What if you are called because no one else would dare answer?

She tightened her grip on the spiral tattoo that coiled her arm, grounding herself.

She had accepted the path. She had not received what it would carve out of her.

Her gaze flickered once toward Naeva, searching for a warning, a farewell, a reason to stay. But Naeva only watched silent and steady at the stones.

There would be no rescue.

Only the path.

The wind shifted, brushing her cheeks with a chill that had nothing to do with the season. Below her, the path wound like a vein through the landscape, narrow, ancient, marked by the weight of every footstep that had come before. She stood at its edge, heart steady but burdened, as if the land itself waited for her to choose. There was still time to turn back. But she knew she wouldn't. The gods had already carved her name into the mist.

***

Ríona turned and followed the mist downward.

"I knew he would."

The trees did not move, yet the mist made room for her. Each step deepened the hush, until even memory walked softer behind her.

The Circle of Judgment lay carved into the hill's flank like a wound that never healed. The path to it was narrow, lined with thorns and twisted rowan. No birds flew overhead. Even the crows, those constant companions of Brú na Bóinne, kept their distance.

The circle itself was older than the language.

Nine stones stood arranged in a ring too precise to be chance. Each was worn, some cracked from time and frost, but they vibrated faintly with the memory of invocation. Ancestral etchings coiled up their flanks like veins, some glowing faintly in the gray light. A shallow basin of black water sat at the circle's center, its surface rippling though there was no wind.

Fareth stood beside it.

He wore no crown, no bone torque, no talismans of rank, only a simple robe cinched with threadbare cord. And yet, none who saw him would mistake his authority. His eyes were carved from the same patience as the land, and his voice held the weight of stones that had listened to ten thousand dawns.

"You've crossed lines not meant for you," he said before she could speak.

Ríona approached without bowing.

"I listened," she said.

Fareth's gaze narrowed. "To whispers that sleep behind the world. The gods do not always intend to be heard. Especially not by those who seek meaning in every silence."

"They came to me."

"They come to many," he said coldly. "And most are driven mad by what they hear."

Ríona didn't flinch. "I was not driven. I was called."

Fareth stepped forward, the basin between them. "And what did they say?"

She breathed slowly, drawing the words from the place between thought and memory.

"They spoke of a heart that was not stone but flame. Buried in the west, beneath the shadow of broken time. They said the world forgets, but blood remembers."

A tremor passed through the circle.

Several of the druids standing at the perimeter stirred. One, a woman with white ash streaked across her cheeks, began muttering protective verses beneath her breath. Another, older, clutched a talisman so tightly his knuckles went pale. "Blood remembers," Fareth echoed. "Old words. Dangerous ones."

28

"They're true," Ríona said.

He looked down at the basin of water, then back at her. "Do you know why the Heartstone of Danu was hidden?"

She remained silent.

"Because it does not forgive."

Ríona blinked. "It's an object."

"No," he said. "It's a vow. Forged by Danu in the days before exile. It remembers every broken oath of the gods and every betrayal of the land. It was sealed away not just for its power, but for its memory."

She stepped closer. "Then why is it stirring now?"

Fareth's voice dropped. "Because something has unsealed it. Something older than you or I. Older than this circle."

A gust passed through, and one of the standing stones groaned.

"You are the anchor of this grove," he continued. "The chants flow through you. The spirits trust you. If you leave, our wards will weaken. The Otherworld will draw closer."

"The Otherworld is already bleeding through," Ríona said. "You've seen the omens. The sun was rising too late. The birds migrating in the wrong direction. Last moon's vision of the sea catching fire."

He hesitated.

"I've seen it."

"Then you know I must go."

The silence stretched. It was not indecision. It was fear.

At last, he said, "You are too young."

"I'm exactly the right age," she replied. "The gods come when the soul begins to turn."

"You think this is a story," he said, with something near sorrow. "You think you're the heroine."

"I think it's already begun," she said. "And I can't stay where the ground is crumbling."

"You don't know what it costs," she said.

Fareth tilted his head. "No," he replied. "But I know what it costs to do nothing."

Ríona turned away. The light was fading now. Or was it her courage that dimmed?

Fareth looked to the stone behind her.

Then, unexpectedly, he turned his back to her.

"You have until moonrise," he said. "If you cross the ring after that, you will no longer be one of us."

She bowed her head, not in submission, but in parting.

And walked out of the circle.

The circle behind her held its breath.

Not one voice called her back.

The silence did not answer. But it opened the path.

The wind did not answer, only carried her breath into the hush where memory held its vigil.

The trees did not stir, yet something ancient pressed close, listening.

Not with ears, but with the silence that comes before remembrance.

The sky had dimmed to its bruise-colored hush when Ríona reached the high glade. This was not a sacred place in any formal sense, no carved stones, no burning lamps, but it was older than the rituals that had tried to define holiness.

***

Here, wind and memory moved through the heather as if they had their own names.

She laid her satchel at the base of a bent hawthorn tree and knelt beside the spring-fed pool that fed the lower stones. Its surface was mirror-black, surrounded by rushes, so still, they might have been made of glass. Her reflection did not show her face.

Only a shadow where her head should be. A blur of wings.

She reached into the water, letting it chill her skin, and remembered the warmth of her mother's hands.

Once, long ago, her mother had brought her to this glade when she was a child. They had sat together beneath the same hawthorn tree before its trunk had begun to twist from age, and she had spoken, not as a priestess but as a woman who knew her end was close.

"You'll be called by flame, little crow," she had said, brushing a loose strand of ember-red hair from Ríona's brow, where it caught the firelight like a vow not yet spoken. "Not because you desire it, but because something old and broken will need you to carry the heat of memory through the cold."

Ríona had not understood then.

Now, she did.

That night had been her mother's last. The fever took her before sunrise. The song she had begun to sing, the one about the dying stars and the tree of fire, had gone unfinished. Ríona had memorized the rhythm but never the final line.

***

The final line would be hers to complete.

The stars are falling, one by one,
Ashes trailing from the sun,
Their names are lost upon the wind,
Forgotten where the light had been.
A tree once burned at world's far edge,
With roots of flame and sky for hedge,
It sang in tongues no crow could speak,
Its leaves were stars that dared to weep.

And still it burns beyond the veil,
Through shattered light, through mournful gale,
The song remains though stars expire ,
The prayer beneath the tree of fire.
Its branches held the final breath,
Of every vow, of every death,
The dusk it sang was not the end,
But fire returned, and stars to mend.
And still it burns beyond the veil,
Through shattered light, through mournful gale,
The song remains though stars expire ,
The prayer beneath the tree of fire.
I was born of ember's sigh,
I will sing when stars all die,
Let my voice be root and flame,
Let the ash remember my name.
And still it burns beyond the veil,
Through shattered light, through mournful gale,
The song remains though stars expire.

And then, the final line came, not from memory, but from within.

***

The girl who sang beneath the fire.

(♪ Song: "The Tree of Fire", see Appendix I)

She drew her knees up, wrapped her arms around them, and whispered to the dark: "I'm afraid."

A breeze stirred though no wind had been felt all day.

Then a scent, charred heather and iron, rose from the earth. And the stillness bent.

From the shadowed branches, a figure emerged, not by steps, but by suggestion. The Morrígan did not walk. She arrived. Her form shifted with the failing light, at once woman, bird, smoke, storm. Hair like woven night. A cloak of feathers that whispered warnings. And in her eyes, no warmth.

Only recognition.

You are not here to be soothed, came the goddess's voice, not aloud, but in the marrow of Ríona's bones. You are here to be reshaped.

"I don't want to be a weapon," Ríona whispered.

Then, be a vow.

Silence pulsed between them, heavier than stone.

Ríona stood, unsteady, and met the goddess's gaze. Her legs trembled, but she did not fall.

"If I walk west," she said slowly, "what will I lose?"

What you no longer need.

"And if I turn back?"

Then, the fire will find someone else. And burn them instead.

The trees bowed. The spring hissed. In the sky, a single star fell.

***

Ríona stepped forward and opened her palm.

The feather she had carried since initiation, black and bound in a red thread, lay there. It twitched though there was no wind.

"I'll go," she said.

The Morrígan's form dissolved, not in retreat, but in dispersal. As if she had never been separated from the air.

Then the spring stilled.

And the pool reflected her face again, eyes glowing faintly like banked coals.

By the time she returned to the grove's edge, the moon had begun to rise, sharp and pale, like a blade waiting for a name.

The cairn behind her stood quiet, lit only by the flicker of ritual lamps. The others had already retreated. Only one figure remained at the gate of stone and shadow.

Naeva.

Her shawl fluttered in the windless air, crow feathers whispering their language. In her hands, she held something small, bound in leather and sinew. She did not speak at first. She simply looked at Ríona with eyes that had seen too many leave, and too few return.

"You're set on this path," she said softly. "Even if the land weeps, even if the gods fall silent, you'll go."

"I have to."

Naeva nodded slowly. "I once said the same..."

CHAPTER 4

THROUGH THE MOURNING TREES

T he forest known as the Mourning Trees was not marked on any map. It marked itself in dreams and in laments. They entered at twilight when the last red flare of the setting sun bled away.

***

Each branch arched overhead like a cathedral ceiling, woven from bone-pale ash and blackthorn. Elder trees, heavy with withered berries, twisted among them, and rowan saplings clung at their roots, guardians against what slept beneath.

Crows watched them from the highest limbs, too still to be natural. Their eyes gleamed, catching the thin light.

With each step forward, the air grew heavier. The scent of damp earth, elder bark, and rotting leaves clogged Ríona's breath. The mist did not drift, it clung, wrapping her ankles like mourning veils.

She touched a fallen trunk, its surface carved not by mortal hand but by time and grief. At her fingertips, a shiver ran up her arm. Grief, vast, ancient, and unyielding, poured into her.

This was a place of remembering. A graveyard without graves.

She pressed her palm flat against the wood, feeling the faint tracing of a spiral, worn almost smooth. Long ago, someone had knelt here, wept here, and left their memory etched in the grain.

She lowered her head. A whisper stirred the mist:

"Do not forget us."

The trees silently wept around her, and Ríona stepped forward, carrying their sorrow woven into her own.

Ainé had once warned her in hushed tones:

"There are names the gods do not speak. Not from fear, but from reverence. Or regret."

The Hollowed. The Husk-walkers. The ones who gave up voice for silence, form for hunger.

Ríona had thought them only tales, old stories wrapped in superstition. But here, where the mist curled like breath withheld and the trees wept without sound, the names no longer felt distant.

They felt close.

The path narrowed where the last oaks grew thick and low, their branches bent not by weather but reverence. No one passed this way unless they meant to leave the sacred circle of Brú na Bóinne behind.

Ríona stood at the final threshold.

The moss-covered arch of stone that marked the grove's edge was older than the cairns and the chants. It had no ancient spirals carved into its face, none visible to most. But as she stepped closer, symbols began to glow faintly beneath the surface, as if the stone remembered being written on.

She paused, inhaled, exhaled. The weight of her years in the circle hung around her like a cloak, her role, her vows, her titles, even her name, all woven into the rites of the priesthood. To step forward was not merely to cross into wild lands. It was to become unnamed.

She reached into her satchel and drew out a small vial of anointing oil, mixed by her own hands at the spring of voices. Carefully, she uncorked it and poured a single drop into her palm.

Then she knelt and touched the stone.

"I am Ríona," she whispered, "but I carry no title here. No circle claims me. No stone binds me. I walk as breath and vow."

The air shifted.

The symbols on the stone shimmered once more, then vanished.

She stood and passed beneath the arch.

The silence beyond was different.

It was not the silence of sacred stillness but of anticipation, the way the world holds its breath just before thunder. Her steps grew softer, muffled by the earth. The ground felt different beneath her feet, less soil, more memory. Each root and rock seemed to watch her.

Behind her, the grove dimmed.

Before her, the Mourning Trees waited.

She did not look back.

Only one crow circled overhead, silent.

She whispered a blessing for the land she had left.

And crossed into the realm where time no longer kept its shape.

***

The deeper she walked, the more the forest bent around her.

Branches arched like ribs overhead, woven so tightly with leaf and shadow that light barely filtered through. The sun was still above the horizon, she could feel its presence distantly, but it might as well have been dusk beneath the canopy.

The trees whispered.

Not words. Not wind. A kind of pressure, like thoughts passed through woodgrain and bark. She couldn't make out meaning, only emotion. Sadness, mostly. Weight. Regret.

The Mourning Trees.

She had heard the name spoken by firelight in stories meant to scare children or humble the prideful. But those tales had only hinted at this place's true nature.

Here, grief had shape.

One tree bent in half as if weeping, its bark split open like a wound. Another had grown twisted into itself, branches clawing downward toward its roots. The air between trunks shimmered occasionally, not with heat but with memory. She saw flickers: a woman holding a child who wasn't there, a warrior bleeding from the chest with no wound in sight, and a pair of hands turning to smoke.

These weren't ghosts.

They were echoes.

Ríona pressed her palm to one of the trees. The bark was warm and pulsing faintly, like a heartbeat dulled by time. She whispered a song she barely remembered, something her mother had sung once while brushing her hair.

The tree didn't respond.

But it listened.

And that was enough.

She walked on.

Bones littered the moss at her feet, some bleached, some freshly broken. Animal, mostly. Small offerings. Sacrifices from ages past. A crow's wing, still wrapped in red thread, lay beneath a root like a discarded vow.

She followed the faint trail of them, items too deliberate to be random: a ring of stones shaped like a spiral, a charred wooden mask half-buried in ivy, and an iron pendant inscribed with a spiral cross, its chain rusted to dust.

Pilgrims had come before her.

Most had not returned.

One tree she passed had seven knives driven into its side, each a different size, each angled downward. A warning or a promise. Or both.

Still, she continued.

The trees whispered louder now. There were still no words, but a rhythm began to build, like a chant without language. It drummed faintly in her bones, matching her steps.

38

She paused at a fork in the trail.

The path was more straightforward to the left, less overgrown, the trees farther apart.

To the right, the path vanished entirely into thorns and mist. But the crow landed there.

Ríona turned right.

The forest did not resist.

But it watched.

And somewhere far behind her, a single tree bent forward as if to weep.

The trees parted without warning.

No slow thinning, no gradual shift, just a sudden opening, like a breath released after too long held. Ríona stepped into a clearing she hadn't seen approaching. The air was warmer here, scented with crushed juniper and smoke.

At the center stood a shallow pool.

Perfectly circular, still as obsidian.

It reflected the canopy overhead so precisely that, for a moment, Ríona felt as though she stood upside down. The trees were below her feet, and the sky was beneath her boots. A single feather floated in the center, unmoving.

She approached the water's edge.

And saw herself.

But not exactly.

The woman staring back from the mirror pool was older, barely, but enough to unsettle. Her hair was longer, streaked with silver at the temples. Her eyes, though still her own, held something sharper behind them, not cruelty, not wisdom, but something quieter.

***

Resignation. The mirrored Ríona didn't blink, didn't breathe. Yet she moved, slowly, deliberately, lifting her right hand, opposite Ríona's, to touch the center of her chest. Ríona followed without meaning to, heat blooming where her palm met her sternum. The reflection opened its mouth. No sound came, but Ríona heard something anyway...

(♪ Song: "Veilbound", see Appendix I)

INTERLUDE I

THE LAST LULLABY

"When the cradle falls silent, the land remembers the song.
Not through sound, but through the roots that weep."
— Old Saying of the Stone Mothers

The fire was low, barely more than embers huddled in the hearth's crook. Shadows stitched the walls with long, trembling fingers. The scent of elder bark and rowan ash lingered on the rush-strewn floor, mingling with the breath of the dying flame.

***

Ríona sat cross-legged, her mother's hands weaving slow braids into her hair, fingers threaded with sprigs of hawthorn and nettle, tokens against forgetting.

Outside, the night moaned against the stones. A thin, restless Samhain wind threaded through the thatch, stirring the red thread woven into the door lintel.

Her mother's fingers faltered.

Ríona held still, pretending not to notice. Her own breath was too loud in the hush.

"Tell me the song again," she whispered.

Ainé smiled faintly, its curve worn thin by fever. She began to hum, the old lullaby sung only in winters when the veil thinned, and the land remembered what it had lost. Her voice was rough but tender, weaving warmth where the fire could not.

The words came slow, shaped more by breath than sound:
"Stars fade, but root remains.
Feather falls, but song sustains.
Ash to earth, flame to sky,
Memory walks when voices die."

Halfway through the last line, her voice broke. The braid slipped unfinished from her fingers.

Ríona turned.

Her mother was smiling still, but her eyes were distant and unfocused. A glisten of sweat marked her brow. Her breathing slowed to a rhythm too deep and final.

Ríona caught her hands and held them tightly, feeling the faint brush of the spiral charm, her mother wore at her wrist, a small disc of crow bone etched with ancient spirals: *"Remember."*

"Stay," she said, the word catching like a thorn in her throat.

The fire cracked once, a sharp, splintering sound.

Ainé's thumb brushed Ríona's wrist in a final, trembling pass. Her lips moved, but no words rose.

Only the shape of a blessing, unfinished.

Then, she was still.

The hearth's last ember flared and guttered, sending a brief trail of smoke that leaned left, toward the Otherworld.

Ríona pressed her forehead to her mother's knuckles. No tears have fallen yet. Only the hollow ache where breath should be.

Somewhere beyond the door, a crow cried once, not mourning, not warning, but remembering.

***

Ríona gathered the feathered braid from the floor, still warm with her mother's touch, and tied it around her wrist with a strip of red thread, a binding vow, as the old ways taught.

Before she rose, she placed a sprig of elder leaves over her mother's heart, a quiet offering, a way for the spirit to find its way through the mist.

She sat through the night beside the ashes, whispering the lullaby's final line again and again until it became a vow:

"I will remember."

(♪ Song: "Lullaby of the Forgotten", see Appendix I)

***

The wind carried no answer, only the hush of all that had been lost.

And still, she stepped forward. For silence was no longer shelter.

It was a vow waiting to be heard. It was a vow.

***

He sat with the harp across his lap, fingers resting on strings that no longer sang.

Not like before.

Not since the hollowed eyes began haunting his dreams.

What use was prophecy if none would listen? What weight did melody hold when the world forgot its tune?

The wind brushed the strings once, unbidden. A low note hummed, like something buried calling out.

He didn't answer it. Not yet.

CHAPTER 5

THE SHADOW IN THE WEST

The moment Ríona crossed beyond the cairn's reach, the air changed. Not with wind, but with memory.

***

The western wood bore no name on maps, only in dreams and warnings. Its trees leaned inward, not from time or wind, but from the weight of what they remembered. Every leaf stilled. Every shadow deepened. The land watched her.

A crow led her still, black wings gliding through the tangled light.

At first, she walked with measured steps, confident. The forest was dense, yes, but she had passed through sacred groves before. She knew the chants. She had the charms.

But by the third turning, the air thinned. Sounds dulled. Her boots sank deeper into a loamy trail that resisted each step. Moss muffled her passage. Trees arched above, rib-like, and began to resemble sentinels rather than shelter.

She paused at a crooked alder. A spiral had been carved into its bark—half-faded, old, unfinished. She touched it. The bark twitched beneath her fingers.

She pulled away.

"This place remembers," she whispered.

The wind shifted. Not ahead. Behind.

She moved on.

The trail narrowed further, flanked now by brambles and root-knotted oaks. The forest no longer felt natural. No animal sounds. No birds. Only the echo of her own breath and the brush of her cloak against bark.

The crow circled once, then vanished into the mist.

Ríona stepped into a grove she hadn't seen approaching. No transition. No boundary. Just a sudden ring of standing stones, ancient and broken. At the center: a basin of ash.

She approached it warily.

The ash wasn't cold.

***

It pulsed faintly with heat. Beneath it, stone shimmered with runes. Her fingers hovered, then traced one.

A voice, low and ancient, rose within her bones.

"Speak the name you will become."

Ríona backed away.

"I have a name," she said aloud. Her voice sounded strange here.

The basin flared.

Visions struck: wings stretched over a field of bones. Fire breaking from the earth. A mountain split with a wound of light. She staggered, fell to one knee. The sigil beneath the ash pulsed again, and her own name slipped from her memory like water from cupped hands.

She reached for the bone charm at her neck—her mother's. It warmed.

"Your name remembers you," she whispered. The ground steadied. The vision fractured and fled.

She turned and fled the grove.

The path back was twisted, uncertain. She passed the same tree twice. Her scratches marked the bark, yet the forest spun in loops.

A sound behind her.

A footstep.

Not hers.

She did not run. She walked with purpose. The trees leaned closer, whispering.

***

A clearing appeared. Unbidden. At its center, another stone. Black. Slick.

She did not approach.

She whispered an old chant, pressing the spiral tattoo along her arm. Her breath steadied.

From the trees, a figure watched.

Cloaked.

Still.

When she blinked, it was gone.

The crow returned. It landed before her, talons curling around a charred branch.

She followed it without a word.

Soon, the forest began to open. Light filtered through the branches. Her breath returned in full.

But the silence followed.

And in the distance, something vast remembered her.

INTERLUDE II

The Heart That Was Sealed

Before the veils thinned. Before fire could speak. Before even the gods were gods, there was the Heart.

It was not born.

It was not made.

It was gathered.

From the breath of Danu, from flame that never cooled, from the echo of the First Word spoken into the bones of the land.

The Heart was memory made manifest.

And memory, once shaped, could shape the world in return. Not by command, but by resonance — every vow, every silence it touched became part of its pulse.

***

The Tuatha Dé Danann named it the Heartstone. It bore no single form. To some, it appeared as a living crystal, veined with gold and shadow. To others, a coil of light in a basin of darkness. In truth, it was not a stone at all, but a threshold: between oath and oblivion, between presence and forgetting.

Long before exile, before the wars that shattered the sky, the gods walked freely among the people. Danu gave the druids their breath-songs, Brigid taught the shaping of flame, and the Dagda bound the rivers to their names. In this time, the Heartstone lay uncovered in the Hollow of Accord, pulsing at the center of all rites. It was not a weapon then, but a wellspring.

Those who touched it did not command — they remembered.

And in remembering, balance held.

When a child was born, their name was sung to the Heart. When two tribes forged alliance, their covenant was braided into its pulse. When the first kings bent the knee to the land, it was before the Heartstone they knelt, for it bore witness—and in witnessing, bound.

But the Heartstone did more than remember. It responded.

The deeper the vow, the stronger its echo. And so it became dangerous.

Not in the hands of gods. Not in the hands of kings.

But in the hands of one who sought to change memory itself.

***

It was not a god who cracked the first seal. It was a druid.

No name remains for him in the chants. None willingly spoken. He was once a keeper of rites, one of the three who had stood at the Eye of the Stone during the last breath-feast of spring. But something hollowed him. A hunger not for power, but for permanence. He believed memory should serve will, not truth.

He performed a rite unbidden, twisting breath and silence together until the flame turned black. He offered no sacrifice but his own name—and in doing so, severed it from the line of witness.

In that severing, the land recoiled — not from violence, but from betrayal. The memory that bound the world had been turned against itself.

The land recoiled. The Heartstone cracked.

This was the Shattering.

The first time a vow unraveled so completely it left the soul behind. He became the First Severed—not dead, not alive, but cut from the roots of all memory. His voice was devoured. His

50

shadow twisted. And in the hollow that remained, silence bred hunger.

From that silence, a question was born — not what had been lost, but what might rise in its absence.

The Hollowed were not born that day, but the seed was planted. A fracture in the weave of remembrance.

***

The Morrígan was the first to answer. She did not rage. She did not mourn. She witnessed. With crow-feather and flame, she walked the circle of forgetting and summoned the gods. Danu wept. Brigid forged three runes of concealment. Lugh turned his gaze westward and said nothing.

Nine veils were drawn across the Heartstone. Nine layers of concealment, silence, and severed names.

The Morrígan laid the final seal. She spoke:

"If the land forgets, the stone will awaken. If the gods grow silent, the stone will call. If one walks west with fire in their blood and silence in their name, the stone will remember."

The Heartstone was buried beneath the Hollow Mountain, its name locked within a ritual only the land itself could remember.

It did not sleep.

It listened.

And though centuries passed, the Heartstone heard every chant that faltered, every rite left unfinished, every child named without witness, every ancestor buried without song. The Heart grew heavy with grief. Not angry—but full. Full of memory. Full of broken threads.

There were signs.

A king fell after swearing peace, his blood turning to ash. A grove bloomed out of season, its fruit tasting of forgotten names. One seer saw her own shadow singing a song she did not know.

The druids began to speak of the Hollowed again, but quietly, as if the words themselves were cursed. They feared the return not of a god, but of a reckoning.

Some believed the Heartstone could be recovered, healed, even wielded. Others believed it should never be touched again, lest it unweave the world.

But it was never about power.

It was always about memory.

Because memory, when broken, does not vanish — it festers. And in festering, it learns how to return.

And memory, once stirred, does not sleep.

***

Now, as the veils thin and the signs return—as the crows fly in unnatural spirals and the rivers sing backward through stone—the Heart begins to pulse again.

Not loudly. Not with rage. But with recognition.

It remembers the shape of silence. It remembers a name sung in red thread and nettle. It remembers a girl who knelt before an altar and asked to remember even if the world forgot.

It remembers Ríona.

And in the darkness beneath the mountain, a flicker of light stirs.

Not because she is chosen. Not because she is powerful.

Because she is listening.

Because she is willing to be changed.

Because memory has found a voice again.

***

And the Heart—not a weapon, but a vow—has begun to beat

CHAPTER 6

ISLAND OF LOST TIME

T he trees thinned, not with warning, but with relief. As if even the forest had held its breath for too long.

***

Ríona emerged from the Mourning Trees at twilight, though she had no sense of how long she had walked. Time had blurred behind her, threaded with dreams, visions, and the echo of a name she still hadn't dared speak. Now, the air opened wide, heavy with salt and memory. Before she stretched a jagged coastline, where the sea met stone in a solemn hush.

She stood at the cliff's edge, her cloak tugged by a wind that did not touch her skin. The sky was muted violet, bruised with unseen weather. There was no sun, no moon, just a long smear of light on the water that might've been dusk or dawn. It offered no warmth.

Below, the sea churned without tide. The waves rose and fell without rhythm, like a heart unsure of its own beat.

A narrow, cracked slate path wound downward to a cove half-veiled in mist. The crow that had guided her so far perched on a twisted yew tree, waiting.

Ríona followed in silence.

The descent was steep, the air thick with brine and the scent of rotting kelp. Yet somewhere beneath that, a sweetness. Wild thyme crushed underfoot. She paused to look. None grew there.

She reached the shoreline, where the stones were smooth and glistening with sea-sweat. No footprints marred their surface. No gulls cried overhead. Even the ocean, for all its movement, made no sound.

Then she saw it.

A boat, moored without rope.

No oars. No sail. Its hull was carved of something dark and ancient, not wood, not bone, but a substance that drank the light and offered no reflection. Along its rim were notches shaped like crow beaks; each one etched with spiral glyphs that pulsed faintly as she approached.

It was waiting for her.

The crow cawed once, sharp, declarative, and flew to land on the boat's prow.

***

Ríona stepped into the vessel without hesitation.

She had crossed more than water. The air no longer belonged to the living.

Even her breath seemed borrowed.

The boat did not rock beneath her. The moment her foot touched the center plank, the sea stirred, not with wind or wave, but with motion. It glided forward, parting the mist like a blade through wool. The coastline vanished behind her, and the world dimmed. Through the fog, a shape emerged, no larger than a hill, no brighter than a memory. An island, unmapped, awaited. The boat touched shore without a sound. Ríona stepped onto sand pale as bone, scattered with spiral-shaped shells that hummed faintly in the sea mist. The air was still, though the ocean churned behind her. She turned to look back, only fog. The boat was gone. No

splash, no ripple. Just her and the island that had waited long
enough.

***

The land sloped gently upward, ringed with towering pines that
grew too straight and too evenly spaced. Their bark glistened like
wet stone, and their needles carried a scent not of resin but of
something older, burned herbs and damp manuscripts. The trees
made no sound, yet their presence pressed against her ribs like a
held breath.

She walked a narrow trail of white gravel that seemed to curve
of its own accord. The shadows here moved strangely, stretching
forward, retreating backward, even though the light above did not
shift. There was no sun, yet there was illumination. No source, yet
clear visibility, a dream's clarity.

Time here... looped.

Ríona paused by a tree where a flower bloomed and withered
within seconds, cycling through life and decay in the time it took to
blink. She reached toward it, but before her fingers could touch
the petals, the plant dissolved into dust and fell upward.

Further along the trail, she passed a pool of water still as glass,
reflecting not the sky but another world, cloudless, with
constellations she did not recognize. One of the stars pulsed as she
leaned closer, flickering like a heartbeat.

Then came the bells.

Not loud. Not distant. But wrong.

They rang in her bones, three chimes, each softer than the last
as if sounding out something forgotten.

***

She followed the trail until it opened into a wide glade ringed by
standing stones. Some had toppled, others leaned together as if
sharing secrets. Grass grew in spirals, pressed down by invisible

feet. Insects darted sideways through the air, only to vanish mid-flight and reappear moments earlier where they had started.

And there, in the center, a tree grew upside-down.

Its dry and twisting roots reached skyward, while its crown burrowed into the earth, blooming faintly with flowers that shone in the dark like stars.

Ríona stood still.

The land hummed, not with welcome, but memory. This was no place for mortals, but a god's remembrance. She was allowed in not because she belonged, but because she had already begun to forget the shape of time.

The air thickened the farther she walked into the glade until each step felt like pressing through the honeyed mist.

At the center of the spiral, beyond the inverted tree, the land suddenly dropped into a shallow hollow. There, fragments of what had once been a temple lay scattered, stone columns, fractured lintels, and pieces of ancient altar stones covered in spiral glyphs now half-swallowed by moss.

Yet their memory endured.

As Ríona stepped closer, the mist shivered, and the broken stones mended themselves in flickers of dream-sight. For a breath, she saw the temple as it had been: tall, luminous, crowned with crow-feathers and woven flame banners.

***

And seated beneath the largest tree, which now barely stood, was a giant.

The Dagda.

Not in the fierce guise of battle songs nor the robed majesty of harvest rites. He sat hunched and weary, cradling a harp too heavy for human hands. His great beard was streaked with silver, his robes muddied, and his hands, once strong enough to shape the rivers, hung limply over the harp strings.

Above him, black fruit hung from gnarled branches, their skins splitting to reveal light instead of seed.

Ríona dared not approach closer.

Instead, she bowed, and the world around her dimmed into a heartbeat rhythm.

***

When she looked up again, the Dagda was fading into the mist, his form unraveling like fog pulled by unseen tides.

A soft sigh shuddered through the earth, as though the land itself mourned his retreat.

From the hollowed stones rose water, slow and sure, pooling at Ríona's feet. It reflected not her face but another.

***

A veiled woman knelt across the pool, her reflection perfect, though nobody stood there in the waking world. Threads of fire wove through her mantle, and the faintest gold gleamed beneath her veil.

Danu.

Mother of rivers, seed of stars.

No voice spoke. No hand reached.

Instead, the water at Ríona's feet stirred itself into patterns, spirals upon spirals, a language written only in movement. And in her mind, she felt the meaning:

"We are not gone. We are not silent. We are not unmade. We are waiting for memory to find its voice."

Tears prickled in Ríona's eyes.

She touched her fingers lightly to the water's surface, and her vision blurred. Where the reflection of Danu had been now stood a figure crowned with antlers, wrapped in a cloak stitched from ash leaves and crow wings.

At first, she thought it was the Morrígan, but no.

This one's presence was lighter. It was fiercer in a way that was not made of death but of vibrant, untamed life.

Aengus, the dream-bearer.

His eyes, pale green like young leaves, pierced her with a sudden recognition: not a command, not a warning, but a trust so absolute that it felt heavier than any burden she had yet carried.

He raised one hand to his brow, then lowered it to his heart, a gesture older than the circle stones, older even than the chants her ancestors had murmured in secret.

And then he was gone.

The pool stilled as mist thickened once more. Ríona sank to her knees at the edge of the hollow, hands trembling, breath shallow. The gods were not dead.

***

They were hidden, folded into places the world had forgotten how to see.

But they remembered her.

And memory, once summoned, was a force not easily undone.

She rose slowly, her legs unsteady beneath her. The mist pulled back, revealing the broken temple stones and the inverted tree.

The air smelled of crushed rosemary and something sharper, iron and cold ash.

Ahead, the path wound downward again.

Deeper into the island.

Deeper into whatever dream memory awaited her next.

She didn't remember lying down.

Only that her legs gave way beneath her.

The spiral path narrowed to a basin surrounded by stone thrones, each one cracked and overgrown yet arranged as though waiting for a council that had long since dissolved into wind and memory.

She collapsed beside a shallow pool fed by no stream. Its water glowed faintly with an inner light, soft as a candle flame, blue as sorrow.

Sleep took her not as rest but as summons.

And she obeyed.

***

She stood in a plain without a horizon.

Ash and grass grew together beneath her feet like fire, and life could not choose who would prevail. In the distance, black mountains floated like ships in the air. The sky held no color, only motion, clouds curved and folded into unfamiliar constellations.

Then came the voice.

Not spoken, not sung, but breathed into her very bones.

"Daughter of flame, Thread-walker, oath-breaker, vow-bearer, do you still remember the name that was not given But earned?"

The sky split like fabric, and a shape wrapped in linen and silence descended from its frayed edge. His eyes were veiled with silver thread. His hands, though scarred, moved with perfect precision as he plucked the air, strings that weren't there but vibrated with ancient sound.

A song formed.

"The crow does not warn. It marks. The flame does not burn. It becomes."

Around him rose fields of crows, each one frozen mid-flight. Their wings outstretched; their eyes open but unblinking. They formed a spiral, each feathered body hovering without motion, suspended as if in the breath between heartbeats.

And from their silence came the rhythm.

"She will give what cannot be given. Speak what cannot be heard. Carry what cannot be held."

The figure's mouth never moved, but the song deepened.

She recognized the voice now.

It was his, the Blind Poet.

Though they had not yet met in waking, she had known his voice in the marrow of dreams since childhood. It was the sound of things just remembered, the chant between prophecy and prayer.

He turned toward her. Though veiled, his face saw more than any unclouded gaze. "Ríona, daughter of nettle and ash, are you still flame? Or have you become the silence that guards it?" She tried to answer, but no words came, only a crow's cry, lodged in her throat. The dream shattered.

***

She woke gasping. The sky above was unchanged, pale, shadowless, endlessly gray, but her hands trembled with heat. Pulling back her sleeve, she found a new mark above the spiral tattoo on her forearm: faint, raw as a burn. Not ink. Not scar. A sigil, unwritten by human hand.

(♪ Song: "Wings Upon the Thread", see Appendix I)

She traced the mark with her thumb, it pulsed once, in time with her heartbeat. The pool beside her had dimmed, its song vanished, but in her blood, it lingered. Ríona rose slowly, her body aching as if she'd fought a battle in her sleep.

The sigil on her arm faded into invisibility as she moved, but she could still feel it, an ember pressed into her skin, pulsing with a slow, insistent rhythm. It was not a burden yet but a bond.

The crow was waiting.

It perched atop a standing stone a short distance away, its feathers ruffled against a breeze that did not touch the grass or stones. It watched her with one eye, tilting its head slightly as if gauging whether she could still follow.

Without speaking, Ríona stepped forward.

The land responded.

From where the crow sat, a path unfolded, not paved with stone or dirt but made of polished bones and river-smoothed pebbles. Each step gleamed faintly, catching light that had no visible source. They formed a spiral pattern, curling outward into a forest of twisted yew trees whose branches wove together into shifting arches.

Every step forward was accompanied by a faint sound, like distant drums, or the island's heartbeat.

She hesitated only once.

At the mouth of the spiral, a standing stone loomed, taller than the others, its surface wrapped in blood-red ivy. As she approached, she saw glyphs etched deep into its face, marks not made by chisel but by the slow patient scarring of time.

One glyph stood out: a spiral within a spiral, split by a single downward line.

She knew it without needing to be told.

A choice.

One path would lead to what she sought.

The other would lead to what she must give up.

She pressed her palm against the cold stone.

The glyph warmed beneath her touch.

In the stillness, a whisper unfurled, not in her ears, but deep within her chest:

"What you carry will be asked of you. What you guard will be tested. To move forward, something must be left behind."

The crow gave a low, rattling call.

Ríona stepped onto the path.

The stones beneath her feet were colder now, and the drumbeat grew louder, not hostile, but inexorable. She was a heartbeat older than her ancestors, even the gods who had cradled the first fires of memory.

She walked until the path, curved out of sight behind a veil of mist.

Just before she disappeared into it, she glanced once over her shoulder.

The standing stones watched.

The inverted tree pulsed faintly in the dim light.

And the island seemed to sigh, not in relief, but in remembrance.

Even here, where time had knotted itself into forgetting, the land still knew her steps.

And it would remember when the time came to ask its price.

Even the stones here remember futures not yet lived.

CHAPTER 7

THE SILENT WARRIOR'S BURDEN

The mist was no longer mist.

It clung to Ríona's skin like a damp cloth, heavy and cold, each breath dragging a chill deeper into her lungs. What light there had come not from any sun or moon but from a soft, sourceless glow that pooled around her feet and gave no warmth.

She tightened her cloak around her shoulders and pressed onward.

The land beneath her boots had hardened into uneven stone, slick with moisture and treacherous. Each step forward felt like she was trespassing into the memory of something not meant to be disturbed. Thorny vines crept across the path, black as old blood, their spines sharp enough to catch even the mist.

Somewhere ahead, the crow called once, a low, throaty sound that rumbled through the damp air.

And behind her, silent as ever, her companion followed.

The Silent Warrior moved with patience born of ritual, his steps placed not by instinct but by ancient choreography. Where she stumbled on unseen roots or nearly lost her footing on the slick stones, he walked as though the land bowed to his passing.

Still, it was not the treacherous ground or the grasping mist that gnawed at Ríona's spirit.

It was the silence.

The oppressive, swallowing quiet that turned each breath into a shouted confession and made every heartbeat sound like an unwelcome drum. Even her thoughts had begun to falter, unraveling into fragmented images of things that had not yet happened: visions of blood on altar stones, of voices she would never hear again.

She shook her head sharply to clear it.

Focus.

The path narrowed further, funneling between two jagged ridges that jutted from the earth like broken teeth. Blackthorn bushes lined the way, their barbs catching at her cloak and sleeves, tearing small rents into the fabric. Some thorns grazed her skin, leaving fine red lines that beaded slowly with blood.

She bit back a cry as one particularly vicious branch tore across the back of her hand, opening a gash that throbbed with immediate pain.

Before she could react, the Silent Warrior was at her side.

Wordless, efficient, he took her hand in his. His touch was firm but careful, his roughened fingers surprisingly gentle as they turned her palm upward to inspect the wound. Without hesitation, he reached towards his belt, tore a strip from the hem of his tunic, and began binding her hand with quick, practiced movements.

Ríona watched him silently, her heart beating too loudly in her chest.

She saw what she had missed in the flickering half-light: the old scars that laced his forearms, crisscrossing in patterns too deliberate to be accidents. Ritual scars. Oaths made flesh. Promises are kept at a cost.

When he finished, he gently pressed her hand toward her chest and stepped away without meeting her eyes.

64

For a moment, she wanted to speak, to thank him, to ask him the questions that had gathered like storm clouds behind her ribs. But the words would not come. The mist swallowed them before they could even form.

She nodded instead, a small gesture, almost lost in the gloom.

He returned the nod and resumed his place a few paces behind her, his presence a quiet shield against the encroaching dark.

Ríona turned back to the path.

The mist thickened once more, but this time, it seemed to part for her slightly, as if, by the small exchange of blood and silence, she had purchased a sliver of the island's reluctant mercy.

She walked on, her wounded hand cradled against her heart, feeling the pulse of it echoing in the stones beneath her feet.

The crow called again, farther now.

Ahead, the trail bent sharply into deeper shadow.

She did not hesitate.

And the Silent Warrior followed.

***

Night thickened around them; a velvet shroud stitched with distant stars.

They made camp beneath the hollow bones of a fallen tree, its roots twisted upward like pleading fingers against the dark. The mist had thinned to damp threads that clung low to the ground, gathering in pools among the stones but leaving the air sharp and cold.

Ríona knelt by the small fire the Silent Warrior had coaxed into being, a low, stubborn flame that snapped hungrily at the damp kindling. She held her wounded hand close to the heat, feeling the sting where blood and sweat mingled beneath the rough binding.

Across from her, the Silent Warrior sat cross-legged, mending the torn edge of his tunic with a bone needle and sinew thread. His movements were steady, mechanical, the work of a man long practiced tending his own wounds, both seen and unseen.

The firelight caught the faint latticework of scars that marred his forearms. For the first time, Ríona allowed herself to study them openly.

Not battle wounds.

Marks of ritual.

Some were the clean, deliberate cuts of oaths taken and witnessed. Others were jagged and uneven, the scars of promises broken and paid for in blood. Each line seemed to hum with its own story; a language older than any tongue now spoken.

She shifted closer, the fire crackling softly between them.

"You carry more than silence," she said quietly, her voice hoarse from disuse. "You carry memory."

The Silent Warrior paused; the needle poised midair.

He looked up, meeting her gaze with a gravity that seemed to anchor the air around them.

Slowly, he set aside his tunic and reached for the blade at his belt, not to draw it in defense, but to lay it bare across his knees, offering its truth.

Ríona leaned forward, studying the weapon.

Along its blade, etched so finely it seemed woven into the metal itself, ran a spiral of ancient spirals marks, ancient letters, telling a story only the old stones still remembered.

With careful fingers, he traced a path from the hilt to the tip, then touched his chest, mouth, brow, and back to the blade again.

A vow.

Broken.

Renewed.

Ríona understood then, not in words, but in the marrow of her bones.

He had been a guardian once. A bearer of sacred songs sworn to protect the rites and the memory of gods who no longer walked

66

the earth openly. Somewhere along the winding path of fate, he had failed, or been forced to betray, and his voice had been taken in that failure. Not by cruelty. By covenant.

A silence not imposed but embraced.

Because some truths were too dangerous to be spoken aloud.

The fire guttered briefly, throwing their faces into flickering shadow.

From the edge of the clearing, the Blind Poet's voice drifted like smoke, a dream-chanted whisper:

"Not all silence is surrender.

Some are shields.

Some are a sword."

Ríona turned sharply, but the poet was nowhere to be seen.

Only the mist moved at the edge of the world.

When she looked back, the Silent Warrior had lowered his head, his hands resting on his knees, a gesture of surrender or supplication, she could not tell.

Without thinking, she reached across the fire and laid her uninjured hand lightly atop his.

They remained like that for a heartbeat, two souls stitched together by loss and stubborn hope.

Then he closed his fingers gently around hers, a silent vow renewed.

The fire crackled louder as if in approval, and the mist pulled back a little more.

Ríona leaned back, feeling the ache of the day settle into her bones, but also something steadier beneath it, a tether, fragile but real.

Tomorrow, the journey will demand more of them both.

But tonight, for a few stolen hours, trust was enough.

***

The morning bled slowly and gray through the mist.

It was not true light that woke Ríona but a thinning of the darkness as if some ancient hand had torn a seam in the veil above. The cold had deepened overnight, sinking into her bones, leaving her fingers stiff and her breath ragged.

The Silent Warrior sat apart from her, perched on a broken column of stone half-swallowed by creeping ivy. His head was bowed, his hands resting loosely on his knees. His sword lay across his lap, a silent sentinel.

For a long moment, Ríona simply watched him.

The fire between them had long since died, leaving only a circle of blackened stones and a faint, acrid scent. In the hush, she could hear the soft rasp of the warrior's breath, the muted whisper of the mist curling through the trees.

A question festered in her chest, bitter as old blood.

Why did he follow her?

She rose slowly, wrapping her cloak tighter around her shoulders, and crossed the short distance between them. The Silent Warrior did not move, though his posture tensed slightly at her approach.

Ríona crouched before him, searching his face.

"What binds you to this path?" she asked, her voice low, raw from disuse.

He lifted his gaze to hers, steady, unwavering, but gave no answer. Only silence, heavy and impenetrable.

Frustration sparked sharp and sudden in her belly.

"You bear the marks of broken oaths," she said, more sharply than intended. "And yet you follow me as if bound by chains I cannot see. What are you, Silent One? Shield or blade? Guardian or executioner?"

Still, he said nothing.

Instead, he placed a hand lightly on his chest and extended it outward toward her, a gesture of offering, of service.

Ríona stared at the gesture, a knot of anger and sorrow tightening in her throat.

Service was not the same as trust.

She stood and turned away, her boots crunching softly over the frost-crusted grass.

From the corner of her eye, she saw him tense, a flicker, barely there, but enough.

Enough to know that her words had struck something raw beneath the surface.

Good, she thought bitterly. Let him feel it.

Ahead, the path twisted into a deeper fold of the hills, swallowed quickly by rising mist.

She started forward without waiting, her wounded hand throbbing with every heartbeat.

Footsteps followed, his, always silent but never absent.

As the mist closed around them again, Ríona tightened her grip on the hilt of her blade.

The journey was far from over.

And trust, once cracked, was a fragile thing.

The mist thickened again as they crossed into the hollow.

No birds sang, no insects stirred, and even the crunch of their steps on the wet grass seemed to swallow into stillness.

Ríona slowed, feeling the hairs on her arms lift. Her skin tightened with the old instinct that warned of watching eyes. She glanced at the Silent Warrior, who had loosened his blade in its sheath.

Something moved beyond the edge of sight.

At first, she thought it was a trick of the fog, a ripple, a shiver. But then the shapes coalesced.

Darkness uncoiled itself from the mist: shadows half-formed into human shapes, their limbs too long, their mouths stretched wide in silent screams. No flesh, no bone, only rags of memory woven into spectral form.

The nearest wraith glided toward her, arms outstretched, fingers tapering into smoke.

The Sluagh had found them.

The Host of the Dead.

Ríona swallowed the surge of fear that rose in her throat. These were not mere ghosts. They were broken souls, drawn to the living by hunger for what they could no longer claim.

***

The nearest wraith glided toward her, arms outstretched, fingers tapering into smoke.

The Silent Warrior stepped between them, blades flashing in a tight defensive arc. His sword met the nearest wraith and passed through. No impact. No resistance.

Only a shuddering ripple that sent a cold shock through the clearing.

The Sluagh recoiled but re-formed immediately, more solid, more real.

They could not be fought with iron.

Only memory. Only will.

Ríona closed her eyes and reached inward.

The sigil on her forearm, born from the Island's blessing, pulsed hot against her skin. She raised her hand, tracing the spiral into the mist.

The wraiths shrieked, not with sound, but with pressure as if the air flinched.

One shadow lunged for her.

The Silent Warrior stepped between them, blades flashing in a tight defensive arc. His sword met the nearest wraith and passed through.

Instinct guided her. She thrust her marked palm forward, and the spiral blazed in the gloom.

The Sluagh shuddered, twisted, and, with a final silent cry, unraveled into motes of light that sank into the earth.

More gathered beyond the stones, flowing forward in a tide of grasping hands and broken faces.

The Silent Warrior moved to shield her, swinging his sword in wide, useless arcs that bought only moments of space.

They could not hold out by force, memory, or truth.

Ríona planted her feet and sang.

Not with her voice, stolen now, sacrificed, but with the resonance of blood and bone.

The song rose from within her, wordless yet shaped by the ancient rhythm stitched into the land: a call to the forgotten, a reminder of what had once been sacred.

The Sluagh faltered.

The shapes began to dissolve one by one, each falling into a spiral of ash and light.

The last to fall was a woman's shade, her face hollow-eyed and sorrowful. She reached out, not in rage, but in longing.

Ríona met her gaze.

In that final glance, she saw the ghost of a name once spoken and a promise once broken, a thread lost to time, now woven anew.

The woman faded into mist, and the hollow was empty once more.

***

Ríona staggered, the effort draining her limbs, her knees buckling.

The Silent Warrior caught her before she could fall, his strong arms anchoring her against the pull of exhaustion.

They remained there for a long time, kneeling together in the damp grass and breathing hard in the aftermath.

Finally, Ríona lifted her head and whispered into the mist: "We remember you."

And somewhere beyond sight, the land itself sighed.

The mist pulled back to reveal a hollow ringed by stones, some broken, some leaning against each other like weary old men. The earth here was soft beneath Ríona's boots, damp with memory rather than rain.

She slowed her steps.

The Silent Warrior followed without hesitation, though his wound from the battle against the Sluagh darkened the edge of his tunic. Blood marked his side, and yet he moved with relentless purpose as if the pain itself had no claim upon him.

At the center of the hollow, a lone standing stone jutted skyward, taller than the rest, etched with spirals so weathered they seemed like scars in the stone's flesh.

Ríona turned to him.

"You should rest," she said.

He shook his head once. A denial is absolute.

Frustration flickered through her, not at his refusal, but at the familiar wall between them. A wall built not of mistrust but of sacrifice.

Without a word, he unsheathed his blade and drove it into the earth at his feet, the impact ringing out like a muted bell. Then he knelt before her, one knee pressed into the damp soil, his head bowed.

Not fealty.

Not submission.

An offering.

Ríona approached slowly, her hand straying instinctively to the mark on her forearm, the sigil gifted by the island's vision. It pulsed with a quiet, steady beat, matching the thrum of the stones and the land's heartbeat.

The Silent Warrior lifted his gaze to her.

In his storm-gray eyes, she saw no plea, no demand, only an unspoken truth:

I am yours to command if you will bear the burden of me.

Her own heart answered before her mind could catch it.

She drew the dagger from her belt, a slim blade of blackened bronze, its edge honed more by ritual than by the need for violence. With a practiced movement, she pricked her thumb and let a single drop of blood fall onto the blade sunk into the earth.

The soil drank it eagerly.

The mist swirled tighter around them, and the spirals on the standing stone flared with faint blue light, pulsing once or twice before fading back into silence.

Binding.

Not by oath forced, but by covenant chosen.

***

Ríona knelt opposite him and placed her uninjured hand atop his outstretched one, palm to palm, flesh to flesh.

"I accept your vow," she said, voice steady despite the tremor beneath it. "And in return, you shall not walk this path alone."

The Silent Warrior closed his fingers gently around hers, sealing the bond.

They rose together as one.

The fire of the ritual faded, leaving only a deeper steadiness between them, a thread woven not by destiny but by shared defiance against what would tear them apart.

***

Ríona retrieved her staff from where it leaned against the stone and turned toward the mist-shrouded path ahead.

The Silent Warrior fell into step beside her, not behind.

Their shadows stretched long across the hollow as they moved forward, no longer merely companions but twin pillars against the tide of forgetting.

Behind them, the stones stood witness.

Ahead, the land waited.

And within Ríona, a new certainty took root:

Some burdens, though heavy, were never meant to be carried in silence alone.

ACT II

The Fire Between Worlds

The flame does not ask who it consumes.

It only remembers who dared carry it.

CHAPTER 8

THE FIRST TRIAL

T he mist peeled back slowly, revealing a landscape torn by
memory.

***

Ríona stepped cautiously into a vast grove where no birds sang, and
no fresh shoots pushed through the soil. Here, the trees grew
sideways, some half-toppled, their roots exposed to the brittle air
like skeletal fingers clawing at the sky. Stones once carved with
sacred spirals lay split as if a great hand had shattered them in anger
long ago.

The air was sharp and metallic, laced with the ghost of ash.
She paused at the clearing's edge, its weight settling in her bones.
This place hadn't just been abandoned—it had been wounded.
The Silent Warrior joined her without a word, his sword loosened
but undrawn. The crow wheeled once overhead before vanishing
into mist. Omen enough. Ríona tightened her grip on her staff
and stepped into the Hollow. Beneath her boots, old leaves
crunched—unnaturally preserved. Her steps echoed longer than
they should, as if the grove feared to remember what had once
been spoken here.

At the center of the clearing stood a twisted altar stone, cracked clean through, yet still upright, stubborn against the slow collapse around it. Ríona approached it cautiously, running her hand across the surface.

The stone was cold, but something stirred beneath the touch, not power, but memory. Flashes of ritual fires, chanting circles, offerings left with trembling hands, devotion turned to ash.

The shiver ran deeper than her skin.

She withdrew her hand, breathing carefully through the rising sense of dread.

"We are not welcome here," she whispered, the words barely shaping themselves in the heavy air.

The Silent Warrior gave a slight nod, an acknowledgment, not a challenge.

They pressed onward, weaving through the skeletal trees, stepping over stones that once formed sacred circles now reduced to ruins. Every so often, Ríona glimpsed remnants of old markings, ancient spirals carved into fallen branches, faded banners tangled among the brambles, the last scraps of a vow broken by those who had once tended this place.

The path narrowed again, funneling them between two leaning pillars.

Beyond, the mist shifted.

Figures waited in the clearing's heart, half-shrouded by fog and shadow, tall, broad-shouldered, their cloaks dark with ochre and ash. Faces painted with spiral marks stared out from beneath heavy hoods.

Not druids.

These were warriors, oath-breakers, remnants of a once-sacred circle now twisted by fear and ambition.

Ríona stopped.

The Silent Warrior shifted into a guarded stance at her side.

Neither moved.

The figures in the mist waited, patient as stone.

The first trial had come.

And the earth, still wounded, watched.

They stepped beyond the leaning pillars into a clearing scarred by old violence.

***

The earth here was scabbed and broken, pitted where, once sacred, fires had been lit and left to gutter. Fallen stones carved with worn spirals formed a loose ring, and within it, shadows moved.

Men and women stood there, cloaked and hooded, their faces painted in ochre spirals and slashes of ash. Some bore spears or staves; others carried nothing, but their posture was threat enough. Warriors, not druids. The oath-breakers Ríona had heard whispered of those once bound to the old circles who had forsaken their vows for hunger unspoken.

At their center stood a figure taller than the rest, his cloak stitched with crow feathers dulled by dirt and smoke.

He stepped forward, peeling back his hood.

A weathered face met her gaze, not cruel, but hardened. Eyes are like flint, cold and sharp.

"You do not belong here, daughter of the hollow songs," he said, his voice rough as a grindstone. "The gods you serve have fallen silent. The Heartstone belongs to the living now, not to the dying."

Ríona stood straighter, the staff in her hand grounding her to the fractured earth.

"I seek only to fulfill the prophecy," she said, her voice carrying across the clearing, steady despite her heartbeat. "Not for conquest. Not for dominion."

The man sneered.

"Words woven by the weak," he said. "The gods are fading because mortals outgrew them. You would see us chained again to withered spirits and empty rites."

A low murmur rose among the others, a current of anger and fear.

The Silent Warrior stepped closer to Ríona's side, his hand resting lightly on the hilt of his blade.

The leader raised his hand, and the warriors were still.

"You carry the mark of the Morrígan," the man said. "You carry blood old enough to wake stones. That alone makes you a threat."

He pointed a finger at her, a slow, deliberate accusation.

"Surrender the path," he said. "Renounce the Heartstone. Return to your hollow mound, or we will unmake you here."

The mist tightened around the clearing.

Ríona felt the land's old grief thrumming beneath her feet, the spiraled stones watching without judgment. Waiting.

She looked to the Silent Warrior and found steady resolve in his storm-gray eyes.

Then she raised her chin and answered.

"I will not turn aside."

For a heartbeat, silence held the world in stillness.

Then, the leader lowered his hand.

And the Red Marked Ones moved as one, breaking from the circle, weapons drawn, faces set with grim finality.

The first trial had truly begun.

***

Blades clashed, and feet pounded across the wounded grove.

The Red Marked Ones surged with grim resolve, and the Silent Warrior met them like a wall of windless fury.

He moved through them precisely, parrying blows, forcing gaps, holding ground. Ríona also fought, striking with her staff, sweeping legs, and ducking under swings of iron and oak.

But there were too many.

80

A spear glanced off her side, sending pain lancing through her ribs. She stumbled back, and one warrior seized her by the arm, dragging her toward the cracked altar stone.

She twisted and kicked, but he was stronger. A blade flashed.

Steel tore through fabric and skin, carving a shallow line across her ribs.

She gasped. Blood spilled.

It struck the roots.

A pulse rippled through the ground.

A force burst from the soil before the blade could strike again, flinging her attacker into a pillar. The air thickened with ancestral tension, and the mist shimmered.

***

Ríona rose, trembling, and without breath, she sang.

No words. Only resonance. Blood. Memory.

The earth answered.

Vines burst upward. Roots twisted free. The grove stirred like a dreaming beast.

The Red Marked Ones froze. Then fled.

The Silent Warrior watched her, sword lowered, awe hidden behind his stillness.

And then, as quickly as it had begun, it ended.

Ríona collapsed to her knees.

INTERLUDE III

THE HOLLOW STIRS

Beneath the roots of hills no longer crowned by sacred fires, beneath cairns whose stones had forgotten the song's weight, something moved.

Not living. Not dead.

***

Hollowed things, stitched together from the tattered remnants of memory, pressed against the thinning veil.

Eyes opened in the darkness, not with sight, but with hunger.

Mouths whispered in forgotten tongues, weaving spells of unraveling, where once songs had woven breath into stone.

The rivers recoiled. The trees bent their branches lower, weeping sap thick as blood. The earth shuddered, trying to remember the songs that once kept such things at bay.

But the forgetting was deep. The old guardians slept.

And the Hollowed remembered.

They remembered the warmth once denied to them. They remembered the thrones lost to time.

And with every breath of mortal forgetting, every broken oath, every song unsung, the Hollowed grew stronger.

The veil shivered.

And somewhere beyond the reach of mortal ears, a crow cried once, sharp, furious, defiant, before the mist swallowed the sound whole.

The grove was silent again.

The Silent Warrior tended her wound in quiet focus. Ríona barely moved.

Her thoughts circled.

What had she summoned? What part of her had cried out and been heard?

She spoke aloud, "This was not song. It was hunger, wearing memory like a mask."

The Silent Warrior gave no answer. Only understanding.

She wrapped her arms around herself and stared into the cracked altar stone.

***

Later, they made a camp beneath a leaning standing stone.

Ríona took her knife, knelt, and carved a small spiral into the dirt.

"I will not let this power unmake me," she whispered. "I will remember who I am."

He watched without speaking, but his breath slowed with her as if he too remembered what had been lost. When she pressed her blade into the soil, he knelt behind her. Not to stop her. Not to join her. Simply to witness. A crow called from somewhere beyond the trees. He looked toward the sound and nodded once, as if acknowledging something unseen.

The Silent Warrior approached. He laid his blade gently across the stone and touched his forehead to the hilt.

Above them, the crow returned.

It circled once.

And dropped a single black feather between them.

Ríona watched it fall and knew:

This vow had been heard.

The grove, at last, exhaled.

A breath long held through sorrow and silence.

Somewhere in the shifting light between branches, the crow vanished.

Not in flight, but into memory.

CHAPTER 9

The Spiral Path

The mist peeled back slowly, revealing a shoreline that defied reason.

***

Illusions, Ríona told herself. Echoes. But a part of her, older and closer to the blood, knew better.

These were not tricks of the island. And not all memories came from the living.

Some were echoes of what had been severed, remnants of those who had forgotten their own names, their own forms.

The Hollowed.

Here, in the breathless hush and weeping stones, Ríona felt them near, not with sight or sound, but with that ancestral knowing that stirred when danger wore the face of silence.

A shiver climbed her spine. Not from cold. From recognition.

They were memories, trapped in the stone and mist, moments snatched from the river of time and left here to rot or weep.

The Silent Warrior drew closer, his hand brushing the hilt of his sword, though no enemy had yet appeared.

Ahead, the shoreline curved inward around a jagged promontory, beyond which the land thickened into something darker, wilder.

The island waited.

Ríona tightened her grip on her staff and pressed forward, the mist closing behind them like a shroud.

Each step dragged at her spirit as if the island demanded a toll not of coin or blood but of memory itself.

She would pay for it.

But not yet.

Not until the island showed its true face.

Waves lapped soundlessly against the stones, but the rhythm was wrong, too fast, too slow, like a heartbeat slipping between worlds. The sea shimmered in colors no mortal sky had ever known grays tinged with green fire, blues so deep they bruised the eye.

Ríona paused at the water's edge.

The beach stretched out before her in both directions, but when she looked closely, she realized it twisted subtly, folding in on itself like a spiral. What appeared straight at a distance looped back nearer than it should, as if time here had forgotten how to march and instead spun slowly in place.

Behind her, the Silent Warrior stood unmoving, a dark shape against the ever-shifting mist. His presence remained her only anchor.

The crow was gone. Even its memory felt thinner.

Ríona turned her gaze inland, where gnarled trees grew at odd angles, their shadows bending away from the setting sun, if it was a Sun, in shapes that seemed to breathe.

She stepped forward.

The ground crunched beneath her boots, not with sand, but with fragments of old bone and shattered shells. Some bore faint carvings, spiral sigils now worn smooth by the relentless passage, or collapse, of time.

As they moved deeper, sounds whispered through the mist.

Children's laughter faded into a woman's weeping. The clashing of swords was swallowed by a soft, aching song. A baby's first cry dissolves into the rustle of leaves.

Each sound lasted only a breath before vanishing.

***

They left the shifting shore behind, following a narrow path where the mist thinned to reveal twisted trees and broken cairns. The ground rose in a slow, uneven incline, each step pulling them deeper into the island's dream.

Before them, half-swallowed by vines and crumbling stone, rose the bones of a hall.

It had once been grand, that much even its ruined shape proclaimed. Stone pillars lined either side, though many had toppled and lay cracked in the grass. Fragments of carved spirals still clung to the surviving stones, and beneath the faint touch of time's ruin, Ríona could almost hear the hum of old rites.

They crossed the threshold together.

Inside, the hall breathed with memory.

The air shimmered faintly, and for a heartbeat, Ríona glimpsed what had been: a roaring fire in a great pit, tables laden with golden vessels, warriors boasting, harps plucking high and sweet under the hands of unseen musicians.

Then, the vision fractured.

The fire guttered. The laughter collapsed into weeping. The harps hung silent and broken.

The hall twisted back into ruin, and only the hollow wind remained.

The Silent Warrior scanned the shadows cautiously, but Ríona felt no threat here, only sorrow.

She moved among the wreckage.

Her fingers brushed the surface of a broken shield carved with the threefold spiral. A flicker of a face, young, proud, wearing a crown of woven oak leaves, flashed in her mind, then vanished.

The gods had feasted here once. Not just gods, kin.

Now, only echoes remained.

She crossed to the far end of the hall, where a heavy door of blackened oak leaned half off its hinges. Vines had grown through the cracks, weaving it shut, but even so, something on the other side seemed to call her name, not in words, but in a pull at the deepest part of her being.

She reached for the door.

The Silent Warrior was at her side instantly, his hand catching her wrist lightly, a question in his storm-gray gaze.

Are you certain?

Ríona nodded.

Together, they pulled the broken door open, and the heavy mist beyond sighed outward, wrapping them in the breath of forgotten ages.

***

The mist thickened around the broken doorway, swallowing all sound but the dull thud of Ríona's heart.

Beyond the threshold, the world changed.

The air grew denser and warmer as if the breath of ancient lungs still exhaled through these ruined halls. The light dimmed, filtered through veils of mist that clung to the shattered stones, and drifted in slow eddies along the ground.

They passed a collapsed archway where faint carvings clung to the stone: spirals, sunbursts, knotwork flowing into itself with no beginning or end.

And then they heard it.

A voice.

Not spoken aloud, not a cry or a song, but a whisper in the blood, vibrating through the marrow of their bones.

"Daughter of stone and sorrow..."

Ríona froze.

The Silent Warrior turned sharply, but there was no figure to face, no enemy to strike.

The voice was not of this world.

It brushed against her mind, ancient and weary.

Another whisper came:

"The weave frays. The old blood thins. Only sacrifice may mend it."

A vision bloomed: a woman robed in green and silver, her face shifting between youth and ancient age.

The voice breathed against her spirit:

"To pass, you must leave behind what binds you to the living."

Voice. Memory. Dream. Choose.

Ríona staggered back, the Silent Warrior catching her elbow.

The vision faded.

The warning remained.

They moved deeper into the island's broken heart.

***

At the center of a sunken hollow, they found a well.

Its stones were smooth, worn by sorrow. Mist swirled within, shifting visions flickering through a child crowned with flowers, a war band riding into mist, a woman weeping by a grave.

Memories.

Ríona leaned closer.

The mist reached for her.

A thousand lives shimmered there, unanchored and hungry.

She extended her hand. The mist reached back. The ground crumbled beneath her feet. Before she could fall, a grip caught her, strong, unyielding. The Silent Warrior. He pulled her from the well's hungry edge without a word.

The mist shimmered once and then stilled. Ríona pressed a hand to her heart, breath ragged. She understood now. The island was no sanctum; it was a snare woven from longing. She turned away from the well and did not look back.

***

They climbed the final rise. At its summit stood a stone archway, hewn from black-veined rock, its surface traced with faintly glowing spirals. At its center, carved in weathered script older than prayer: *Only in silence shall the path open.*

Ríona placed her palm to the stone. Visions flared, her childhood, her songs, the first time she heard the spirits call. To pass, she knew she must relinquish what had always been hers.

Her voice. Her gift.

She stepped back and dropped to her knees. And sang.

***

It was not a song of power, but of farewell, a parting, a letting go. The mist curled tighter, listening. And when her voice at last fell silent, utterly, reverently, the stone door opened.

The Silent Warrior touched her shoulder once in reverence.

Together, without a word, they crossed the threshold into the unknown.

And the island exhaled, closing the path behind them.

CHAPTER 10

The Vision of the Gods

"The wind holds its breath before the forest burns.
Even silence has a shape,
and it waits."
— *From the Whispered Verses of Brú na Bóinne*

B eyond the stone door, the mist parted like a breath released after centuries, as if the island exhaled her passage into a more profound mystery.

***

Ríona stepped through the stone door and found herself in a vast cavern, not carved by mortal hands but shaped by the slow dreaming of the earth itself. Above, the ceiling arched into darkness; below, the ground rippled with veins of crystal and blackened roots that pulsed faintly with unseen life.

The cavern glowed with a ghost light, neither fire nor moon, but a soft illumination that seemed to emanate from the very stones.

And within that glow, she saw them.

***

Statues, she thought at first, tall, magnificent figures standing in solemn array across the cavern floor. But no artisan's chisel could have wrought such terrible beauty. Flesh and spirit mingled in their forms: some shining with a golden luster that caught the breath, others dulled and cracked like fallen idols.

These were not statues.

They were gods.

The Tuatha Dé Danann, the Shining Ones.

Silent. Sleeping.

Ríona moved slowly among them, heart pounding in her throat.

Here was The Dagda, his massive frame crowned by a great club that touched the cavern floor, his eyes closed as if dreaming of harvests that would never come again.

There was Brigid, her hair a river of flame frozen mid-fall, a forge hammer clutched loosely in one hand.

Beyond them, Lugh of the Long Arm stood poised as if at the cusp of battle, his spear lowered in slumber.

Near the cavern's far wall, woven into a tangle of roots and starlight, sat a throne, not carved but grown, upon which slumped a figure draped in faded green and silver.

Danu.

The Great Mother.

Her head bowed, her hair cascading in dull strands over her shoulders, her breathing so faint that Ríona wondered if it was breath or merely the last sigh of a dying world.

The Silent Warrior remained at the threshold, wary but silent.

Ríona stepped forward alone.

Inside the silent hall, she heard it: the drip of water and the slow thrum of stone, remembering the song.

She passed close to the sleeping gods, feeling their dreams brush her skin, fragments of battles, laments, and unfulfilled vows.

***

Danu stirred. Her eyes, clouded yet piercing, opened and met Ríona's. No words passed between them, but something older than language moved in the stillness.

94

Ríona felt it, not a message, but a weight. A gravity older than stone. The gods were not dead. They were waiting.

Waiting for a choice. Waiting for her.

***

The throne thrummed beneath her feet, pulsing in rhythm with something vast and unseen. And then the visions came, not flashing, but unfolding. They layered over the cavern like twin dreams: one of a world that might be, the other of one that never was.

A tremor passed through the stones beneath her, and the mist shimmered with possibility.

Her breath caught as the first vision unfolded.

She was not merely being shown what could be — she was being asked what would be allowed to become.

The cavern around her shimmered.

***

The First Vision: The Gods Awaken

The Dagda rose, laughter booming over the hills. Crops ripened in a single breath. Rivers sang. Brigid's flames leaped to life, lighting new temples. Lugh's spear seared the sky.

Mortals bowed beneath sacred trees. Oaths renewed. The gods ruled.

And those who questioned fell silent.

Choice withered beneath divine brilliance. Freedom bent.

High in a black-feathered temple, Ríona sat crowned, weighed by the sorrow of a world that gleamed, and groaned under unseen chains.

The vision cracked.

***

The Second Vision: The Gods Fade

The gods slept on.

Crops withered. Wars burned.

But mortals endured.

A girl sang to a broken forge. A poet carved myths from hunger. A boy spun stories from nothing but the breath of stars.

No oaths. No temples. Just like, messy, wild, fiercely free.

Ríona walked among them, a crow-cloaked wanderer, no queen, no priestess, bearing memory as a whispered seed, not a sword.

The visions faded, but their ache remained. They had not simply shown what could be, they had revealed the price. One world shimmered with wonder, yet its beauty came bound in chains. The other burned with freedom, carved in ash and sorrow.

Both bore her name.

One path offered peace bound by obedience, a world remade but ruled. The other, freedom seared by uncertainty. She could not save both gods and memory. But she could choose which would endure.

To save memory was to accept the world's imperfection — to trust it to remember, and to forget, on its own.

Both demanded a decision, not of power, but of self.

***

The cavern returned. The throne hummed, its silence louder than any chant. At the threshold, the Silent Warrior knelt, waiting without pressure or plea.

Ríona pressed her palm to the spiral etched on her forearm. The mark pulsed once, not with command, but with remembrance.

And she chose.

Not dominion. Not retreat.

She chose memory.

She withdrew her hand from the throne, the decision sinking into the bones of the cavern as surely as it sank into her spirit.

Danu's cracked lips curved, not a full smile, but the sorrowful blessing of one who knew the cost of hope.

96

The mist stirred, thickening and rising, carrying her choice through the roots of the world.

The way forward opened, not with triumph, but with a sigh of memory.

Danu's lips curved, a ghost of sorrow, a ghost of blessing. The mist stirred. The way forward opened.

***

The corridor beyond the throne was narrow, its air thick with breath unbreathed. They walked in silence, footsteps swallowed by the hush. The passage widened into a chamber sculpted from the roots of the world, walls pulsing faintly with buried memory.

At the center hovered the Heartstone fragment, a shard of pure light, slowly turning, casting ripples of gold and violet across the floor. It pulsed, calling.

Ríona stepped forward, her heart hammering. Visions flickered at the edges of her mind, battles and blessings, songs and funerals, every thread of existence woven into motion. She hesitated.

Then, she reached out.

***

Her fingers closed around the light, and the world exploded into memory.

She stood suspended in a river of stars, each droplet a breath, a prayer, a death. Pain sliced through her, not of flesh, but of spirit. Lives flashed past: kings crowned and broken, mothers mourning, children dreaming.

The Heartstone tested her. Rule or wander. Command or remember.

She let the torrent pass through her. She did not resist. She endured.

And when the burning ceased, the Heartstone settled into her palm, its song folded into her blood. Her hand now bore its mark, a spiral of living light.

She trembled. She was no longer fully mortal. Nor yet divine.

Something between.

A bridge. A memory.

She turned from the altar. The mist thickened once more, curling like breath, beckoning her toward paths unmarked by time.

And she walked forward, carrying the first light of the world within her.

CHAPTER 11

THE SACRIFICE

T he mist thinned as they climbed the last rise, revealing a hollow cradled in the island's bones. The land sank into a shallow bowl, ringed by standing stones so ancient that their surfaces had worn smooth under the weight of endless years. Each stone leaned inward as if the earth had drawn breath once and never exhaled.

***

At the center of the Hollow, the ground was bare and slick with dew, save for a single monolith, taller, darker, and untouched by lichen or time.

The air here thrummed, not with sound but with a pressure that tugged at the blood and marrow, pulling at memories, unspoken fears, and forgotten promises. It was the heartbeat of something far older than the gods themselves, the raw pulse of a world where sacrifice was not asked but inevitable.

And beneath that pulse, a familiar thread stirred, not in the world around her, but within.

A tension at the base of her spine.

A flicker behind her eyes that saw not form, but omen.

The Morrígan did not call to her. She waited.

Not as patron or protector, but as witness, the kind who marked whether a vow would hold or break beneath its own weight.

Ríona did not speak her name. She did not need to.

Some bonds do not require summoning. Only remembering.

Ríona slowed, feeling the resistance with every step. Each pace forward was a quiet act of will, as though the land weighed her soul and found it lacking.

Beside her, Eolan moved like a ghost; his sword sheathed, but his hand was never far from the hilt. The Silent Warrior's gaze, what little could be read from it, was wary but unwavering.

Breasal, the Blind Poet, walked unerringly at her side, his blind eyes half-lidded, his fingers brushing the strings of the harp strapped to his chest. He hummed softly, a wordless song, but even that faint comfort was swallowed by the Hollow's gravity.

They crossed into the circle. And the world shifted.

The Hollow did not echo.

It received. It remembered. And now, it waited to be fed.

The Silent Warrior tilted his head, listening not with ears but bone. He touched two fingers to the dirt, then to the spiral carved into his bracer. A gesture older than language.

The mist beyond the stones thickened into a wall, cutting off the sky, the land, and the memory of anything beyond this place. Inside the circle, time itself fractured, Ríona glimpsed moments flashing at the edge of vision: a red sun setting behind shattered towers; a river boiling with the weeping of crows; a lone woman kneeling on cracked earth, her mouth open in a scream she could not voice.

Then the visions faded, leaving only the thrum, the stones, and the waiting silence.

Ríona placed her palm against the dark monolith at the center of the Hollow. It was warm and pulsing as if something beneath the stone was alive and listening.

She closed her eyes.

The sacrifice had already begun.

The ground beneath the hollow quivered, not from any earthquake but from something deeper, older. The standing stones shuddered in their ancient sockets, and from their trembling shadows rose a shape.

***

It emerged without sound. A tall figure draped in tattered black feathers and smoke; its form wavered at the edges like mist caught between worlds. Its face was hidden beneath a hood of woven darkness. Still, its presence was undeniable, weighty as the ancient stones, sharp as winter stars.

It did not walk toward them. It simply was, one-moment mist, the next a being formed of sorrow and law.

Eolan stepped protectively before Ríona, his hand falling to his sword, but the Blind Poet touched his arm, stilling him.

"Not an enemy," Breasal murmured, his voice carrying the tone of ancient recognition. "A guardian."

The figure raised one long, branch-thin arm and pointed toward Ríona, not with malice, but with grave expectation.

It spoke without voice. The words did not pass through the air; they unfolded directly into Ríona's mind, heavy and slow as stone doors opening.

"None may pass untouched." "The hollow demands offering." "Not blood. Not flesh. Soul for sight. Breath for burden. Voice for vision."

Ríona's throat tightened. Though no hand touched her, she felt the threads of her being pulled taut, her songs, her prayers, her invocations, all bound together by the living breath within her chest.

The Silent Guardian bowed his head once as if offering sorrow before demanding duty.

Breasal turned his blind gaze toward her, voice low, almost reverent. "Nothing is taken here," he said. "Only what is freely given."

The mist around the Hollow deepened, turning the world beyond the stones into a blank, waiting for silence.

Ríona placed her hand once more upon the central stone. The warmth had deepened, thrumming now with the pulse of her own blood.

She understood.

This was not punishment. This was the price of knowing.

The sacrifice was not death. It was a transformation.

And it had always been waiting for her.

Ríona let her hand fall from the stone, the warmth clinging to her palm like a living memory.

***

The Silent Guardian remained unmoving, its feathered form fading and sharpening with each breath she took as if it existed halfway between possibility and finality.

In the stillness, Ríona understood the bargain fully now, not just its price, but its meaning.

Her voice was not merely sound. It was her prophecy, song magic, and power to weave the spirit world into mortal hearing. It was the last tether of her mortal self, her humanity stitched to the world through breath and utterance.

To lose it would be to lose the primary way she *touched* the world.

The Blind Poet stepped forward; his harp silent against his chest. His voice, ragged with something more profound than mere sadness, filled the Hollow.

"Once, the first druids walked the world with sight unhindered by breath. They sang no songs aloud. They carried no names. They saw the rivers run backward and the stars weep silver blood.

But to see thus..." He touched his throat lightly. "…is to unmoor oneself from all things."

His blind eyes turned toward her, fierce and sorrowful.

"Once given, you will not take it back."

Eolan said nothing, only standing at her side, a steady, silent pillar.

The mist around them began to coil as if the Hollow itself was listening, waiting for her heart to speak where her lips could not.

Ríona closed her eyes.

She saw the Heartstone pulsing with promise and peril in the darkness behind her lids. She saw the faces of the gods, Danu weeping into the soil, the Dagda leaning heavy on his club, and Brigid casting sparks into a dimming world. She saw the wars that would come if balance was not restored, the rise of mortal will be unchecked, and the fading of all things sacred.

Her voice was small compared to that.

When she opened her eyes, the choice had already been made.

She stepped forward, head high, toward the Silent Guardian.

"I offer," she said, the last words she would ever speak aloud.

∗∗∗

The Guardian bowed, and the hollow pulsed once, a vast inhalation, as if the island drew breath to receive her gift.

The Guardian raised both arms, and the standing stones answered.

A low vibration filled the hollow, not sound, but a trembling that reached deep into bone and memory. The mist above them spiraled inward, forming a wide circle of shifting light as if the heavens themselves leaned close to witness.

The ground beneath Ríona's feet grew warm, and the monolith at the Hollow's center pulsed with a slow, ancient rhythm. It beat in time with her heart, faster, until she could no longer tell where she ended and the land began.

The Silent Guardian stretched forth one elongated hand and, from its shadowed palm, unfurled a long black feather, iridescent and sharp as a blade.

It drifted through the air, impossibly slow, and hovered before Ríona's lips.

She understood what must be done.

Her hands lifted without command, fingers brushing the feather's shaft. It was cool and alive, humming with the breath of the Otherworld. As she closed her eyes, she felt threads weaving themselves from her chest outward, invisible cords of song and spirit, connecting her voice to all she had been and might yet become.

And then, with a single breath drawn deep into her lungs, she pulled the feather across her lips.

No pain.

No blood.

Only a feeling, like a great bird had taken flight from inside her, tearing free from flesh, bone, and soul.

She gasped, but no sound came.

Her voice, her power to call, sing, and command the spirits, was gone.

Not stolen. Given.

Freely. Fully.

***

The mist roared in silence, folding inward like a closing bloom. The standing stones flashed with ancient light, one heartbeat, then darkened again.

The Silent Guardian lowered its arms and bowed deeply as if before a queen.

Ríona staggered, but Breasal caught her gently by the elbow, steadying her without a word. His face was wet with silent tears.

Eolan knelt, bowed, his hand pressed to the earth in reverence.

The ritual was complete.

104

And Ríona, though she stood among her companions, had crossed a threshold none could follow.

The hollow fell utterly still.

Even the mist seemed to bow around Ríona, parting slightly to grant her space to breathe this new air, to wear this new skin. But when she tried to speak, to offer comfort to her companions, to reassure herself, only silence rose from her parted lips.

A strange calm settled over her.

The world had not ended. It had only changed.

Slowly, she lifted her gaze, and the Hollow answered.

***

She no longer saw as before. The stones shimmered with threads of memory, bright and fading, some taut, others frayed and broken. The mist was no longer merely damp air but woven with the breath of generations, sighs and songs, and whispered regrets. Every blade of grass sang a soft note of belonging, of grief, of defiant survival.

She turned to Breasal and Eolan.

And she saw them as they truly were.

Breasal was surrounded by faint streams of silver, threads of dream stuff connecting him to unseen places and unseen pasts. Eolan burned like a steady fire, orange and iron-red, his oath and his sorrow twined so tightly they could no longer be undone.

And beyond them, in the mist, Ríona glimpsed more: figures standing at the edges of vision, ancestors, gods half-forgotten, creatures shaped from starstone and river song, all watching, all waiting.

The Hollow had accepted her sacrifice.

And in return, it had given her the one thing no blade or prayer could offer:

Truth.

Raw and unwoven.

Ríona swayed slightly, the sheer immensity pressing against her, but she did not fall. The earth seemed to rise gently to meet her step as if the land bore part of her weight now.

She had crossed the veil. And there would be no crossing back.

CHAPTER 12

THE HIDDEN PATH

T he path sloped downward, narrow and twisting, as if it had been carved not by mortal hands but by the slow dreaming of the earth itself.

Ríona led them, her steps sure despite how the ground shifted underfoot, moss and stone blending in ways that defied natural order. Though no words passed her lips, her presence filled the narrow way, a quiet beacon woven from silence and will.

The mist thinned here, not vanishing but settling close to the ground, coiling like living breath between the roots and stones. Above them, the boughs of ancient, gnarled trees knitted together into a dark, low ceiling. Their trunks were twisted into shapes almost human, arms stretched upward, faces half-formed in the bark, mouths frozen mid-cry.

The air grew colder.

Breasal walked a half-step behind Ríona, his hand trailing lightly over his harp strings, the faintest vibration in the silence, a guide not of sound but of memory. Eolan guarded the rear, his hand resting on the hilt of his sword, eyes sharp beneath his fur-lined hood.

No birds sang. No insects stirred. Only the soft scuff of their boots and the occasional rasp of breath marked their passing.

The deeper they moved into the vale, the heavier the air became, thick with unseen presences, with old griefs soaked into the very roots of the trees.

Ríona's new sight revealed thin veils between worlds: Echoes of processions long gone, faint lights flickering like will-o'-the-wisps between the trees, whispered prayers left hanging in the branches, caught there like forgotten songs.

Each step forward pressed them deeper into the woven memory of the land, into a place where even time seemed reluctant to tread.

Far ahead, somewhere beyond sight, a low pulse beat, slow and rhythmic, calling them onward.

The Heartstone's pull was growing stronger.

And so, they descended, swallowed by the Hidden Vale's deepening embrace, knowing that turning back was no longer possible.

No path marked their way, only the hush between breaths.

Even the roots seemed to pause, listening.

Then the silence cracked like memory returning.

Something shifted, soft, invisible, ancient.

Not wind. Not omen. But presence.

As if the vale itself held its breath, remembering.

They felt it in their marrow, in the quiet between steps.

Not warning… not welcome… but waiting.

The deeper they went, the less the path resembled anything made for mortal feet.

The air grew dense and expectant as if the land had drawn breath and was waiting for memory to quicken again.

Shapes began to move at the edges of vision. They're not fully formed, but they're not imagination either. Faint outlines: a woman with a broken harp slung across her back; a warrior missing half his face, his shield held close against his chest; a child cradling a twisted staff of rowan wood.

They were not truly there, yet they were not absent either.

Ríona could feel them now with a clarity that burned. Each spirit was an echo left behind by those who had once walked these paths, champions, seers, guardians, bound still by love, duty, or unfinished sorrow.

***

Some reached out long, thin hands toward her as if pleading. Others simply watched; their faces carved from the same silence that now filled her.

Breasal hesitated once, brushing his hand lightly through the mist where a figure wept against a tree. The spirit did not turn but left behind a trail of cold that clung to his skin.

Eolan kept his sword low but ready, moving sideways across the path whenever the mists grew too thick, shielding Ríona's flanks like a silent sentinel.

The spirits did not attack. They did not hinder.

But their presence pressed heavily upon the companions, weaving a tapestry of grief and warning across the trail.

Ríona's new sight picked up more. Above the murmuring spirits, faint symbols hung in the air, ancient spirals etched in light and fading shadow: *"Courage," "Memory," "Price."*

She slowed before a crumbled cairn marked by one such sign. Kneeling briefly, she touched the ground in silent acknowledgment, not to beg passage, but to honor those who had walked here before and paid their own tolls to the unseen.

The mist seemed to part a little at her gesture, and the pulsing heartbeat of the Heartstone grew stronger, steadier.

They pressed on, weaving between the watchful dead.

Soon, they would face a choice, and the land would demand more than remembrance.

It would demand *a decision*.

The path widened unexpectedly, spilling into a clearing ringed by twisted stones and ancient, fallen trees. The mist coiled in thick braids here, weaving across the ground like rivers of forgotten breath.

At the center of the clearing stood three archways of stone. Each leaned slightly, weathered and broken, but through each, a distinct trail wound into the mist beyond, three paths leading into the unknown.

Each path looked the same immediately, narrow, shrouded, half-swallowed by roots and fog, but as Ríona's sharpened sight brushed over them, differences began to bloom.

The first path pulsed faintly with a soft golden light, warm and inviting, like the memory of hearth fires and sung prayers. The second path rippled with silver mist, constantly shifting, never the same shape twice, like water fleeing from cupped hands. The third path loomed dark and steady, shadow pooling thick at its entrance, its stones cracked with veins of crimson like old, slow-bleeding wounds.

Breasal stopped just behind her, his hands tightening on his harp.

Eolan surveyed the paths with narrow eyes, distrust written plainly across his face.

"Which way?" he asked softly, though he must have known by now that no answer would come from Ríona's lips.

Instead, Ríona closed her eyes, reaching not with sight or hearing but with the deeper thread now woven through her being, the thread of sacrifice, memory, and trust.

The first path sang of comfort; of things she yearned for. The second whispered of change, the shifting tides of fate and uncertainty. The third thrummed with pain and burden, the weight of choices that could not be undone.

Her chest ached with longing for the golden path, to walk into the arms of memory, to find rest.

But she knew. The actual path was never the one of ease.

Her hand lifted, steady and unwavering, pointing to the third archway, where the darkness pooled and the stones bled.

***

Eolan said nothing, only tightening his shield strap across his back. Breasal bowed, murmuring a soft blessing in a tongue older than kings.

Together, they stepped through the arch of shadow and into the path that would not forgive mistakes.

The mist closed behind them, and the clearing, the choice, vanished like a breath of winter air.

The path narrowed, the stones and roots clawing at their feet as if trying to pull them back, to keep them from the sorrow ahead.

A thin, keening sound began to rise from the mist, faint at first, no more than the sigh of distant winds but growing sharper, rawer, until it scraped against the soul itself.

They entered a grove where the trees stood brittle and bare, their branches reaching out like broken arms toward a sky they could no longer touch. The ground was littered with fallen leaves that had long since turned to ash, crumbling underfoot without a sound.

***

And among the withered trunks moved the mourners.

Banshees, dozens of them, drifted between the dead trees, their forms almost human but thinner, paler, woven from mist and memory. Their faces were veiled by their long, matted hair, which was twisted with frost. Their wails twisted the air, not as shrieks of terror but as deep, heart-wrenching laments for things long lost and never recovered.

Ríona felt their sorrow pierce her chest like thorns, not for herself but for the gods. For the fading of names once spoken with reverence, for the shrines abandoned to moss and time, for the songs unsung.

The banshees did not block the path or welcome the travelers. Their weeping grew louder as Ríona passed among them, her silence a painful mirror to their endless mourning.

Breasal pressed closer to her, his harp trembling against his chest with sympathetic sorrow. Eolan moved cautiously, his hand ever near his blade but not drawing it, knowing instinctively that to strike, there would be a greater wound than any enemy's sword.

As they walked, Ríona's sight revealed glimpses within each banshee: visions of their former lives, priestesses abandoned in lonely groves, seers silenced by kings, mothers mourning children who forgot the old ways.

The weight of their grief bent the trees, soured the soil, and frayed the very mist into ragged threads.

Yet Ríona did not flinch.

She carried her own silence now, a sacrifice freely made, and in that silence, she bore witness to theirs.

Slowly, the wailing softened as they passed. One by one, the banshees turned their veiled faces toward Ríona, not with hatred but with a hollow recognition.

Not every sorrow demanded a voice. Some were honored simply by being seen, being carried onward.

When they reached the far edge of the grove, the banshees' cries faded into a long, lingering sigh that folded back into the mist.

Ríona touched her hand lightly to her heart and bowed once toward the weeping grove.

And the path, for the first time since they entered the island's depths, seemed to open more willingly before them.

***

They had not gone far beyond the Mourning Grove when Breasal stumbled.

It was not clumsiness. It was as if the earth itself had reached up to seize him, pulling his spirit briefly out of step with his body.

He dropped to one knee, a hand bracing against the damp, root-tangled ground. His harp, usually silent against his chest, thrummed a discordant note that shivered through the mist like a broken thread.

Ríona and Eolan turned at once.

Before either could reach him, Breasal lifted his head, his blind eyes wide, but they did not see the present.

They were gazing into something far beyond the veil.

Breasal's mouth moved, forming words, but no breath was carried. Visions crowded around him, unseen to all but Ríona: flashes of light and shadow, a river of blood flowing backward, the Heartstone splitting into mirrored shards, a hand, hers?, reaching out and finding nothing.

***

He clutched at the harp, drawing from it a trembling sequence of notes that sketched a shape in the mist: A towering door of stone and bone, sealed with runes, and the faint, sorrowed face of someone who should not betray but would.

Breasal's voice finally broke free, hoarse, and cracked.

"Beware the one who weeps not when all others mourn," he rasped.

"Beware the hand that offers comfort when the wound is still open."

His words echoed strangely in the mist as if the land caught and twisted them.

Then, as suddenly as it seized him, the vision released him. He slumped forward, panting, the harp strings stilled.

Ríona crouched before him, her silent gaze steady, her hand lightly touching his shoulder.

Breasal shook his head slowly, sorrow etching deep lines across his face.

"I see too much now," he whispered. "And yet... not enough."

Eolan scanned the mist ahead, his face grim. They had faced the grieving dead and the demands of the land, but this warning spoke of betrayals yet to come, dangers woven not from rage or sorrow but from false kindness.

The way forward was no longer just a path through the Otherworld.

It was a path through trust itself.

They rose together, slower now, more wary, and pressed onward toward the beating heart that still called from the deep mist ahead.

***

The path narrowed into a deep cleft between walls of gnarled roots and stone, the mist pressing so close it clung to their faces and filled their lungs with every shallow breath.

The air turned colder, sharper, biting into flesh like unseen claws.

At first, the resistance was subtle: Loose stones shifted treacherously underfoot. Roots rose from the earth like grasping hands. Shadows moved just beyond the edges of sight, whispering half-familiar voices that tugged at their minds, promises, regrets, names long buried.

But soon the land abandoned all pretense.

A twisted branch snapped out like a serpent's strike, grazing Eolan's shoulder with a force that would have broken lesser men. He grunted but did not falter, drawing his blade without hesitation.

Ahead, Ríona felt the earth lurch, how a body spasms in pain. The ground cracked open in spiderweb fractures, forcing her to leap forward, the hem of her cloak snagging on a jagged stone.

Breasal stumbled again, but this time Eolan caught him, pulling him clear of a tangle of blackened vines that writhed like blind worms.

The path was testing them.

114

No spirits, no enemies of flesh, only the land itself, alive with the buried fury of forgotten oaths and forsaken memories.

Ríona's silence became her shield.

Where sound could have been twisted, used against them, her voiceless presence moved like a blade through the mist, steady, unbroken.

She pressed onward, guiding them with the surety granted by her sacrifice. Every step forward costs something: a sliver of strength, a fragment of memory, a small surrender of the warmth that clung to mortal skin.

The trees above seemed to close in, branches clawing the mist into ragged ribbons. The stones underfoot bled thin trails of mist that coiled around ankles and wrists, seeking to root them in place.

But Ríona would not yield. Nor would those who followed her.

When they emerged from the cleft, breathing hard, the mist lessened slightly, and the ground levelled into a narrow, open plain.

The island's fury receded, not in defeat, but in grim acknowledgment.

They had been tested.

And they did not break.

The mist thinned further as they stepped onto the plain, a long stretch of land where no tree grew, no bird sang, and no root dared rise from the soil.

***

It was a place carved out of the Otherworld by sacrifice alone.

Ríona slowed, her breath steady but her limbs aching with the journey's toll. The silence within her, once raw and hollow, now pulsed with quiet strength, a presence all its own.

Before them, across the vast stretch of empty land, something shimmered faintly through the last low veils of mist.

A structure.

Ruined, broken, but unmistakably ancient.

A great circular temple, half-swallowed by time and earth. Its pillars leaned like old warriors bearing unseen wounds. Its once-smooth stones were cracked with the slow bleeding of forgotten magic.

Above its fallen arches, pale lights flickered, not stars, but something older, some echo of the first fires lit by hands now dust.

And deep within its heart, Ríona could feel it, pulsed the slow, steady heartbeat of the Heartstone.

Not loud. Not commanding.

Simply waiting.

She glanced once at her companions.

Eolan's face was grim but resolute, his hand resting lightly on the hilt of his sword. Breasal stood silent, his harpstrings humming softly with tension and sorrow.

No words were needed.

Together, they crossed the barren plain, their shadows stretching long behind them, pulled toward the place where fate, gods, and mortals would meet.

And above them, unseen beyond the veil of mist and broken sky, the stars shifted, as if leaning closer to witness what would come

CHAPTER 13

THE LOST GODS

"The river does not mourn the bend.
It simply turns."
— Proverb of the Fifth Shore

T he plane ended abruptly.

The earth gave way to a broad, broken plaza of dark stone, half-buried under creeping moss and the weight of centuries. Pillars leaned at reckless angles, cracked and bleeding fine trails of mist from their wounds. Carvings, spirals, knots, circles of suns, still clung to the surfaces, though time had worn them into the barest of outlines.

***

Before they rose, the ruin of the temple.

It had once been a place of immense power, Ríona could feel it vibrating faintly underfoot, like the last shudder of a harp string after the music had ceased. Now, it was a hollow carcass of what had been: walls crumbling into heaps of stone, sacred arches splintered into broken ribs framing the gray sky.

Mist swirled thicker as they approached the threshold. It pooled in the broken doorway, resisting entry as though even the Otherworld mourned what had been lost here.

Ríona stepped forward without hesitation.

Her silence somehow made the temple's grief more bearable, her breath carried no song to disturb the ruins, and her steps left no echo to remind the stones they were empty.

Eolan followed at her side, sword drawn now, but pointed downward in a gesture of respect. Breasal entered last, his hand pressed to the strings of his harp as if to still their trembling.

Inside, the ruin yawned wide.

The interior was a circle open to the sky. The floor was a mosaic of shattered tiles, once vibrant with color, now faded to a dusty memory of blue, gold, and crimson. The faintest scent of ash lingered in the air, sharp and bitter, clinging to the edges of memory.

At the far end of the broken circle, atop a dais cracked in three places, something pulsed faintly in the mist.

The Heartstone.

Not a perfect jewel, not the blinding relic of legend, but a rough, blackened mass, as if fire and sorrow had fused it into a single, living thing.

Its slow pulse beat in time with Ríona's heart.

And deep in her bones, she knew:

This was no simple retrieval.

This was communion. Confrontation. And cost.

The gods had not abandoned this place entirely.

And neither had what remained of their grief.

They crossed into the ruin's heart.

The broken stones shifted beneath their boots, whispering of years and hands long gone. Once proud and wide as the sky itself, the temple walls had collapsed inward, leaving only jagged teeth of stone framing the mist-heavy heavens.

At the center of the ruin rose a dais, fractured, leaning, its surface veined with deep, ancient cracks. Shards of what had once been sacred icons littered the ground: fragments of a sun disc, the broken haft of a giant club, and a handful of tarnished torcs twisted into unnatural shapes.

These were not just relics of worship. They were memories made of stone, now broken and weeping dust.

Ríona's gaze fixed on the Heartstone.

It lay cradled atop the shattered altar, a rough, black mass, its edges jagged like flint, its surface pulsing with slow, stubborn life. It was not beautiful, not perfect, but alive.

And it called to her.

***

The pulse of the Heartstone resonated in her bones, in the hollow space where her voice had once lived. It did not demand. It did not plead. It simply existed; a truth woven into the very marrow of the world.

Breasal stopped a few paces behind her, his hand clutching the harp as if to anchor himself against the pull. Eolan placed himself between her and the broken archways beyond, guarding against dangers seen and unseen. However, his posture carried more reverence now than readiness.

The chamber breathed, a slow inhalation of mist, memory, and sorrow.

And from the edges of that breath, something began to stir.

Shadows moved among the fallen stones, shapes forming where none had stood before. Not solid. Not whole. But present.

Faded echoes of something vast and old and grieving.

The gods had not left. Not entirely.

Their broken memories remained, woven into the shattered stones, waiting for someone brave, or foolish, enough to listen.

They were not gone.

Only folded into silence, waiting to be named again.

And the chamber, listening still, heard her bones remember.

She heard no voice, yet something within the silence reached for her.

Not a command. Not even a promise.

Only presence, deep, wordless, and watching.

The mist within the ruin thickened and pulsed, responding to the slow heartbeat of the Heartstone.

***

As Ríona stepped closer to the shattered dais, her sight sharpened beyond mortal limits. Shapes began to emerge from the mist, faint, fragile as moth wings, yet carrying the solemn gravity of ancient mountains.

She saw them.

The echoes of the gods.

Danu, the Mother of Waters, stooped with grief, her once-flowing hair tangled with brambles, her hands still cupped in the eternal gesture of offering. The Dagda stood behind her, his great club cracked down the center, his chest heaving with a breath he had been trying to release for a thousand winters. Brigid knelt nearby, her cloak smoldering with dying embers, her hands calloused and broken from trying to rekindle forgotten flames. Lugh's shadow flitted at the edges, limping, his bright spear broken, his laughter reduced to a silent, watching stillness. And Aengus, the eternal youth, hovered like a pale wisp, not fallen, but faded, his hands empty, reaching for songs the world no longer remembered.

They were not truly alive. Nor were they truly dead.

They were the memory of themselves, stitched to the bones of the temple, woven into the slow, steady breathing of the Heartstone.

Each turned toward Ríona, or what remained of them, and their faces were marked not by anger but by deep, wordless sorrow.

They had not abandoned the world.

The world had abandoned them.

And now, standing before their broken reflections, Ríona understood:

The Heartstone was not merely a relic of power.

It was a grave.

A remnant.

And perhaps, a beginning.

If she dared to claim it.

She took one step closer, not yet a choice, but a reckoning.

The gods did not beckon. They bore witness.

Around her, the temple seemed to lean in. Stones strained as if trying to hear what her silence might mean.

And still, the Heartstone pulsed. Not faster. Not louder. But deeper.

Like a second heartbeat waiting to be joined.

The mist thickened again as Ríona approached the Heartstone.

It coiled upward in slow spirals, wrapping around the shattered pillars and broken icons like incense in a forgotten shrine. The echoes of the gods, Danu, The Dagda, Brigid, Lugh, and Aengus, shimmered at the edges of sight, flickering like dying stars.

For a moment, silence reigned.

Then, without wind or breath, their voices stirred.

Not words spoken aloud. Not a song carried on the air. But a weaving of thought, sorrow, and memory that pressed against Ríona's mind, heavy and deliberate.

"Child of stone and blood," came the first whisper, Danu's voice like rivers freezing under winter's breath.

"Bearer of the old songs," Brigid murmured, her voice crackling like embers buried deep in ash.

"Seeker of broken truths," rumbled The Dagda, each word a weight falling through the earth.

The gods' echoes encircled her, weaving a tapestry of sorrow and warning.

"The Heartstone is life," Lugh whispered, fainting as light slipping through a ruined roof. "But it is also a parting."

"To claim it," Aengus said, almost tender, "is to walk between the worlds. To wear a crown unseen. To bear a name unsung."

Ríona closed her eyes.

***

The meaning flooded her, not just in words, but in sensation.

If she took the Heartstone, she would never again walk fully among mortals. Her voice was already sacrificed. Her ties to the ordinary world would wither. She would become something other, a bridge, a guardian, a myth still breathing but no longer wholly human.

There was no anger in their warning. Only sorrow.

They had once borne such burdens themselves. They knew the price.

They offered her one final chance, to step back. To leave the Heartstone untouched, to let the old power fade, to remain bound to earth, breath, and kin.

No blame would follow her.

No curse.

Only the slow forgetting of gods who had once shaped the skies.

The mist tightened, waiting for her answer.

***

The mist folded in closer as Ríona neared the Heartstone.

Each step felt heavier, not because of distance but because of the weight pressing against her spirit, a slow, grinding sorrow that wore at the edges of her resolve.

She paused at the foot of the shattered dais.

The echoes of the gods hovered around her still, their faded forms rippling like reflections in broken water. No longer warning, no longer pleading, only watching.

Ríona reached toward the Heartstone, her fingers trembling despite herself.

And the visions came.

Not forced. Not inflicted.

122

Revealed.

She saw herself standing again in Brugh na Bóinne, a woman of flesh, breath, and laughter. The warm hearth fire. The songs sung beneath stars. The faces of those she loved, blurred now but achingly familiar.

She saw a life in which she never crossed the threshold into the Otherworld, where she married, and where she bore children who did not hear the breath of the gods in the wind.

A life of forgetting.

A life of peace.

And she saw another life, the one this choice would carve.

A woman half-seen, half-remembered. A name is spoken in prayers but never answered. A guardian unseen, unheard, known only in the way the mist clings to standing stones at twilight.

Neither life would be painless.

Both required sacrifice.

Tears welled in Ríona's eyes, unbidden, sliding silently down her cheeks.

For life, she would never live.

For herself, she must now leave behind.

But still, she did not step back.

Her hand hovered above the Heartstone, her body trembling with sorrow and certainty.

The gods' echoes bowed their broken heads.

They had known this pain, too.

And now, it was hers to bear.

She did not know what the gods would see in her choice.

Only that she could not walk backward through silence.

The world would change, and so would she.

Ríona stood alone before the shattered dais, the Heartstone's dull pulse matching the heavy throb of her own heartbeat.

The echoes of the gods watched, no longer guiding, warning. Only witnessing.

The mist wrapped around her ankles like the hands of forgotten ancestors, clinging but not pulling, whispering but not pleading.

Slowly, she lifted her hand.

The world seemed still, even the shallow breath of mist, even the weight of sorrowed stone, everything held in fragile suspension.

There was no voice to name her act.

No right to shield her.

No prayer to bargain with.

Only the silence she had earned.

She stepped forward, crossing the last distance between who she had been and who she must become.

***

The Heartstone flared, a slow, sorrowful light, less like fire and more like memory reigniting itself after a long forgetting.

Ríona's fingers brushed the stone.

It was cold.

It was burning.

It was everything the gods had left behind, and the mortals had already begun to lose.

Her vision blurred, not from pain but from its raw gravity, the feeling of being seen by every river, oak, and star that had ever marked the turning of seasons.

The broken gods bent low, their fractured forms bowing not in dominance but in mourning and acknowledgment.

Ríona closed her eyes, letting the last thread of her old self slip free.

Not slain.

Not lost.

Offered.

And the Heartstone accepted.

The world trembled, but not with fear.

It was as if the stone itself remembered what it meant to be whole.

As if the old vows, scattered like ash across centuries, stirred once more to listen.

Above the silence, the breath of the land deepened, drawn not in pain but in awakening.

Something had returned. And it would not be forgotten.

The mist recoiled, then spiraled inward, drawn toward her like threads sewing a new, unseen tapestry around her being.

The world was no longer the same when she opened her eyes again.

Nor was she.

The earth trembled as Ríona's hand settled fully upon the Heartstone.

It was not a violent shaking but something more profound, a slow exhalation from the world's bones. The broken stones of the temple groaned. The cracked mosaics underfoot flared faintly with the memory of old light, tracing out faded spirals and suns that no mortal had tended in a thousand years.

The mist above their heads churned, thickening into whorls that stretched up toward the unseen heavens as if weaving a thread between the mortal and the divine.

The echoes of the gods pressed closer, their hollow forms brightening for one last moment.

Danu lifted her sorrowful face. The Dagda rested his great hand upon his broken club with solemn pride. Brigid's eyes blazed once more with the last spark of her endless fire. Lugh's shadow straightened, the memory of his bright laughter stirring for a heartbeat. Aengus brushed the empty air with unseen fingers, scattering one last invisible song into the mist.

They did not speak. They did not need to. Ríona understood.

The rite had already begun. Her silence, her surrender, her step beyond the bounds of mortal knowing, it had been received, acknowledged, woven into the pattern. She was no longer just Ríona of Brugh na Bóinne.

She was the thread drawn between gods and mortals. The watcher at the threshold. The silence that remembers.

Beneath her palm, the Heartstone pulsed stronger, its rhythm sinking into her blood, her breath, her becoming.

The mist around the ruin condensed into bright motes, then burst outward in a slow wave, carrying the memory of this moment across the island, into the rivers, into the stones, into the sleeping bones of the hills themselves.

***

And when the light faded, Ríona remained, standing alone on the dais, her cloak stirring in the wind no other could feel.

Behind her, Breasal lowered his harp with a trembling hand.

Breasal knelt beside her, fingers trembling on the edge of his harp. "I saw it too," he whispered. "The forgetting. It crawls through the chords—I can't play the old songs without hearing silence at the end. I used to think prophecy was a gift. But what if it's just memory grieving too loudly?"

Eolan sheathed his sword and knelt, head bowed.

The temple had accepted her.

The world had shifted.

And the true road, the road that led to survival and transformation, had finally begun.

Ríona did not speak as they turned from the temple.

The vision still shimmered behind her eyes, not like a dream, but like a newly sealed wound.

The gods had not chosen her. Not truly.

They had simply remembered what it meant to be forgotten and passed that burden to her.

What she had touched was not power. It was memory sharpened to a blade. A knowing too vast for one spirit to carry unchanged.

126

And yet, she would carry it.

Not to save the gods. Not to restore shrines.

***

But to keep alive the thread, so that the world would not forget itself entirely.

CHAPTER 14

THE BETRAYAL

T he path away from the ruined temple sloped downward into a thick mist that erased the world by degrees. Each step swallowed the landscape behind them as if the island wished to forget what had been awakened.

Ríona led them in silence, her hands steady, her breath measured. The Heartstone pulsed against her chest, a slow, resonant thrum like the heartbeat of something not wholly mortal. It did not race with fear or hope. It beat with inevitability.

Behind her, Breasal walked lightly, but his head bowed lower with every pace. The harp slung across his back quivered faintly, strings whispering under the damp breath of the mist though no fingers touched them.

Further back still, Eolan followed, yet not as he once had.

His footsteps had lost their quiet vigilance and grown heavy and uneven. Every few paces, the soft rasp of his sword against its scabbard broke the hush, a restless hand brushing too near the hilt. It was not readiness. It was conflict.

The air pressed down on them, dense and heavy with something unspoken. The mist did not merely obscure sight; it thickened in the mouth, clogged the breath, and weighed against the ribs.

Ríona felt it coiling behind her ribs, too, Not fear. Not even sorrow.

Change.

A shift she could neither halt nor soften.

She cast a glance over her shoulder once, not to check the path but to see them, Breasal, burdened by the knowledge he could not sing aloud. Eolan, wearing the silence like a blade, did not know how to sheath.

The fellowship that had borne her across river and glen, that had kindled fires against the night, was fraying before her eyes, And she could no more mend it than she could deny the truth she now carried.

The mist parted slightly ahead to reveal the next threshold: a narrow bridge of ancient stone spanning a chasm of darkness so deep even the mist refused to fill it.

The bridge waited like a blade laid flat across the void.

Ríona tightened her grip on the Heartstone's chain.

There was no returning to what had been.

Only the crossing remained.

And not all would cross unchanged.

The mist pressed tighter around them as they neared the bridge.

The stones beneath their boots became slick with unseen moisture, and every step sounded louder in the smothered world, a drumbeat against the hush.

Ríona moved steadily forward, but she felt the widening distance behind her. Once woven tight by firelight and trust, the bond between them now frayed with every footfall.

Breasal kept pace just behind her, his head still bowed. The occasional tremor of harp strings stirred faint echoes in the mist. But Eolan lagged, not from weariness but from hesitation.

Ríona could hear how his boots scuffed the stones, pausing too long between steps. She could feel it, a snag in the weave of their fellowship, a stitch being pulled loose.

She slowed slightly, enough to draw them closer without turning, without acknowledging the fracture directly. But it did not close.

Instead, she caught the soft hiss of leather as Eolan's hand slid across the hilt of his sword once again.

Not readiness.

Not defense.

A subconscious preparation for something he could not yet name or could no longer deny.

The mist twisted between them, alive with old magic, with memory. The air around the Heartstone seemed to resist him, though no visible force stirred.

Ríona tightened her grip on the relic beneath her cloak.

The Heartstone's slow pulse had deepened, thrumming a rhythm not meant for mortal ears. It was a song of endings, of severings.

She heard Breasal draw a sharp, silent breath behind her. Even blind, he saw more than most, and he, too, had felt it.

The bond that had carried them across river, glen, and dream was buckling under the weight of what lay ahead.

Ríona pressed forward.

***

The bridge loomed fully before them now, its ancient stones slick with mist, suspended over a chasm that seemed less a wound in the land than a wound in the world itself.

She did not look back again.

Some choices were made in silence.

Some betrayals, too.

As they stood before the bridge, the mist peeled back in slow, reluctant strands.

It arched narrow and trembled across a void that swallowed all sound and light. No stars pierced the gulf beneath them, and no wind stirred the mist above it. Only the stones endured, worn smooth by centuries of forgotten footsteps and perhaps forgotten choices.

Ríona stood at the bridge's mouth, the Heartstone's weight dragging harder against her chest. Not physically heavier, but spiritually, undeniably so. As if the bridge itself demanded a toll from her soul before she could pass.

Breasal paused at her shoulder, one hand lightly resting on the harp that had, until now, remained silent.

Behind them, Eolan halted, his breath harsh in the tightening stillness. The distance between them felt measured not in paces but in chasms.

For a long moment, none of them moved.

The bridge shimmered faintly under the mist, not with magic or welcome.

But with judgment.

Ríona felt it coil through her blood: This was no mere crossing of land. It was a crossing of fates.

She reached beneath her cloak, her fingers brushing the Heartstone. Its pulse throbbed once, hard and sure, and for the first time, she understood.

To step forward was to accept the cost. To remain was to forfeit everything.

She exhaled slowly.

No prayers. No second thoughts.

The gods had made their silence known. The choice was hers alone now.

With a single step, Ríona placed her foot on the bridge.

***

The stones felt colder than death. Older than memory.

132

Behind her, Breasal shifted, his harp strings humming once in recognition. This low, mournful note did not break the silence but deepened it.

Eolan did not follow immediately.

His hesitation was a wound Ríona could feel, even without looking.

She took another step forward.

Mist coiled around her ankles like restless hands.

The Heartstone beat against her sternum: slow, steady, remorseless.

She did not turn back.

Some bridges demanded a crossing blind.

Some demanded a crossing alone.

The bridge narrowed further; stones slick with the breath of the abyss yawning beneath them.

Ríona pressed onward, each footfall a choice carved in silence. Behind her, Breasal followed, his harp strings trembling faintly as if plucked by unseen hands, the song of sorrow not yet sung.

But Eolan... Eolan hesitated at the threshold.

The mist coiled about his boots, reluctant, as if the island itself questioned him.

He paused at the edge, the stone beneath his boots cold and questioning.
He had followed her through shadow and betrayal, but this step required more than loyalty.

It demanded surrender.

And Eolan, forged in silence and blood, had never learned to give.

Ríona stood ahead, changed. Not distant but becoming something beyond his reach. He felt the fracture not in his mind but in his marrow, the part of him that once believed silence was shield enough.

Still, he lingered, between oath and uncertainty, between following and falling away.

***

He watched Ríona's back, saw the Heartstone's faint pulse beneath her cloak, and felt something ancient and raw fracture within him.

She had changed. Or perhaps he had remained behind, clinging to vows made on simpler nights before destiny bared its jagged teeth.

The bond he had sworn upon, the woman he had bled for, they were slipping beyond reach, beyond mortal grasp.

His hand moved almost without thought.

A sharp rasp, leather on leather, as he drew his sword halfway from its sheath.

Breasal turned slightly at the sound, a blind man sensing the storm long before it broke.

Still, Ríona did not turn.

Still, she trusted.

That final thread pulled taut, quivering between them.

Eolan stepped forward, not in anger, hatred, or desperation.

He surged toward her, one hand outstretched, not for her, but for the Heartstone, the only thing he believed could anchor her back to them.

The mist recoiled at his movement. The bridge shuddered beneath his boots.

And as his fingers brushed the edge of the relic's hidden gleam, the wards flared.

Invisible forces burst outward in a violent shock, hurling him back.

Eolan cried out, not in pain, but in heartbreak, as he staggered, sword clattering from his hand, skidding across the stone into the mist.

***

He fell hard onto one knee, and his head bowed.

The sound of his breathing filled the hollow space where trust had lived.

The mist swallowed his shame, wrapping around him like a mourning shroud.

And Ríona, standing unmoved, closed her eyes, once, against the ache behind her ribs.

The silence did not end. It deepened.

Not to crush them, but to hold space for what words could not reach.

In that breathless stillness, something waited, soft as sorrow, steady as truth.

There were no battles here. Only endings, betrayals that needed no voice to wound. The silence that followed was not absence; it was presence, thick and unmoving, as ancient as the stones beneath their feet.

Eolan remained kneeling, head bowed, as if whatever force had cast him back had scraped him clean from the inside.

And Breasal moved.

Slowly, reverently, he stepped toward the center of the bridge, toward the wound that had opened between them all.

His blind eyes lifted slightly, searching not with sight, but with something more profound, memory, grief, understanding.

The harp on his back stirred as he drew it forward, cradling it against his chest. His long, calloused, and sure fingers found the strings without hesitation.

He did not strum a bold note. He did not summon a song of triumph or sorrow's rage.

He simply played.

A single line, trembling and thin as a breath through cold reeds. A note so soft it seemed more felt than heard.

The melody wove through the mist, A song of campfires long dead, of laughter, carried on rivers now run dry, of nights when three souls believed the stars would guide them home.

It was not a lament. Nor a hymn.

It was memory itself, stitched into sound.

Ríona stood at the far edge of the bridge, still turned away, her hand resting lightly on the Heartstone beneath her cloak.

The music wrapped around her shoulders like a cloak woven from every vow ever made, every oath ever broken.

Eolan remained unmoving.

But as Breasal played, a shudder passed through him, the kind of grief too deep for tears, too broken for anger.

The harp strings quivered, breathing life into the mist, the stones, and the silence.

For a heartbeat longer, the bridge became what it had once been, not a place of endings but of crossings.

And then, with a final brush of trembling fingers, Breasal let the song die.

No lingering echoes.

No resurrection.

***

Only the simple, brutal mercy of silence.

He bowed his head over the harp as one bent over the grave of something beloved and lost.

The mist closed again, gentle and indifferent.

And they stood upon the bridge, no longer three bound together, but three shadows crossing into different tomorrows.

When the final note of Breasal's song faded into the mist, something inside Ríona stilled. Not healed. Not comforted. Simply... settled.

She turned to face them at last. Eolan remained where he had fallen, still kneeling, the mist curling around him like penance. His sword lay abandoned near the bridge's edge, half-lost to the fog.

136

Breasal stood farther back, harp silent in his hands, its strings quieted by will, not weariness.

Ríona's gaze moved between them, the warrior undone by fear, the bard shackled by memory. She loved them both. But love, here, was not enough.

She stepped forward. Not to offer her hand. Not to raise Eolan from his knees. But to walk the final span of space that choice demanded. Her boots scraped the stone, a mortal sound on a bridge balanced between worlds.

Eolan looked up, eyes bloodshot, lips parting as if to speak, but no words could reach across what had already fallen away. Ríona, once a believer in the sacredness of oaths, knew now: some vows were meant to end. Some loyalties broke not through betrayal, but through destiny.

She bowed her head, not in pardon, but in mourning, and walked past him.

***

A breath passed between them, no more than a thread, sharp as separation.

Eolan did not follow. He bowed low, forehead to stone, yielding to a wound no blade had carved.

After a moment, Breasal turned and walked behind Ríona. Together, but changed.

Never as they had been.

And behind them, the mist folded closed, erasing the path back as if the gods themselves agreed: mercy lies not in return, but in forgetting.

And the mist, sensing farewell, softened.

It did not part, but it yielded enough for the leaving.

She did not look back.

Not toward the one who stayed behind.

Only forward, into the breathless hush of what waited.

The mist thinned as they neared the shoreline.

The stones underfoot grew rougher, rawer as if the island itself shed its illusions the closer they came to leave.

At the water's edge, the small boat waited, half-drawn onto the shingle, bobbing gently in rhythm with the slow, mournful tide.

No one spoke.

There was nothing left to say.

Ríona stepped forward first, her hand brushing the weathered wood of the boat's prow. The Heartstone pulsed against her chest, steady, sovereign, indifferent to the fracture it had witnessed.

Breasal followed, his harp slung back over his shoulder, silent but whole, carrying the memory of what was lost.

As they climbed in, the boat rocked under their weight. Mist clung to the gunwales, whispering against the sides like forgotten prayers.

Only when they had settled did Ríona lift her gaze to the shore.

Eolan stood there, not near, not far. A shape blurred by mist, as if he had already become part of the island's sorrow.

His sword remained at his side, untouched.

His head was bowed, but whether in grief, regret, or simply resignation, she could not say.

Ríona did not call out.

She did not reach across the gulf that had opened between them.

Some chasms were meant to remain unbridged.

Breasal pushed the boat gently from the shore.

***

The current caught them, slowly but sure, pulling them away from the island's weeping stones.

As the mist closed behind them, Eolan's figure faded, not swallowed, not erased, but folded into the silence that would always lie between them.

Above, the sky sagged low and violet, starless.

138

Ahead, the river unwound like a thread into the unknown.

The river widened behind them, folding into dusk like the end of a song never finished.

Mist wrapped the boat in trailing ribbons, clinging to the hull like old hands unwilling to let go.

Breasal rested his hand gently on his harp, not to play, but to feel it echo softly with the weight of unspoken things.

Ríona turned her head slightly, not toward Eolan, but toward where he had stood—now nothing more than a shadow fading into the shoreline.

He had not followed. And she had not asked.

There was no bitterness in the distance now. Only recognition.

Some things could only walk so far together. Some partings were the price of becoming.

***

The boat rocked gently, and above them, the first stars broke through the veil of dusk, flickering like memories too old to name.

Ríona exhaled. The sound did not carry. It did not need to.

The path ahead no longer required witnesses—only the courage to carry what could not be returned.

And Ríona, holding the Heartstone to her chest, let the silence settle within her, Not the silence of grief.

The silence of becoming.

INTERLUDE IV

THE SILENCE BETWEEN SONGS

The song came in fragments. Not in Ríona's voice, nor Breasal's. It drifted in the stillness between waking and dream, a thread she could not grasp, only follow. She saw a grove burning. A shrine crumbling. And a girl who could not remember her name.

She had once been called Nessa. Once. Before the veil thinned before the grove burned.

What had been sacred once now whispered in ash — not gone, but left behind, waiting to be remembered.

In her final year, she tended to the shrine alone. The others had fallen to the fever, wandered west, or grown tired of praying to gods who no longer answered. Nessa had stayed, not from faith but from memory. She remembered the sound of the river before the drought. She remembered her mother's chant, which always ended in a hush.

The chant was simple, carried more in breath than voice:

By ash and root, by wing and flame, let silence not take what memory claims. Let the wind remember the names lost to stone. Let the dark yield to the breath that sings.

She would kneel at the stone circle, offering hawthorn and black feathers. The rite was performed at dawn, barefoot, always facing east. No flame was allowed, only voice, only memory.

Over time, even this began to slip. One day, she forgot the third line. The next, she left the feathers but no name. Then, she stopped facing east.

When the wind changed, the birds left. Even the crows.

At first, she sang louder to fill the quiet. Then softer. Then, not at all.

It began as forgetting, the sacred names, the order of the offering, the way back from the circle of yews. Some nights, she would wake with her own name just out of reach. Each time she tried to call it back; it rang hollower in her mouth.

One morning, she found the shrine empty, though she did not remember placing the offerings. Her hands were stained, and her breath felt borrowed.

She stopped singing.

They came when the mist no longer moved. Not as beasts. Not as spirits. Just shapes, faint and folding, as if they had once been real and were trying to be again.

They did not walk. They pressed. Like memory does in the back of the mind, persistent, soft, and ruinous.

She did not run. There was nowhere left to go.

They circled her, not touching, not speaking. But she felt it, that pull. The lure of vanishing. Of silence made permanent. It would have been easy. Easier than remembering.

One reached forward, not with a hand, but with absence. Her name flickered in her mind, distant and decaying.

But then, something moved within her. Not a god. Not a flame. Just a sound.

A single note.

She sang.

Not to call power. Not to defy death. But to remind the world that she had once existed — and remembered.

Not to be saved. Not to call down power. But to remember.

The shapes recoiled. Not with pain. With distance. As if the song made them less sure of their place.

They did not take her. But they did not leave her untouched.

She awoke days later at the edge of a lesser grove, skin cold, name half-formed on her lips. An old man tending sheep found her and led her back to the village, though he would not speak of what he saw in her eyes.

She spoke little after, not from fear but from weight. What she had seen, she could not forget. What she had nearly become, she could not name.

Now, she walks at the edge of sleep. Between rites half-formed and melodies half-forgotten. A voice neither wholly hers nor wholly borrowed.

Not Hollowed. Not whole.

Remembered only in the silence between songs.

Some say Nessa's grove still stands, hidden in a fold of time, wrapped in ivy and hush. Druids no longer seek it; bards sometimes speak of it in their laments. A place where silence can devour the self unless you carry a song strong enough to name the dark.

Breasal once dreamt of her in the deep hours, a girl with a silver thread around her wrist, walking between stones older than the gods. He did not know her name, but his harp refused to play until he whispered a song for the forgotten.

It lasted only a minute. But the string it touched hummed long after.

The same note would later echo in Ríona's chest, long after the dream had passed, unclaimed.

CHAPTER 15

THE FINAL TRIAL

T he boat drifted toward the far shore, where mist bled into the land and shapes shifted like half-remembered dreams. The river's gentle yet relentless current bore them forward without oars, without will.

***

Ríona sat at the prow, her hand resting lightly over the Heartstone hidden beneath her cloak. Each thrum of its pulse seemed to draw her deeper into the unseen fabric. She felt the world thinning, the weave of mortal certainty unraveling.

Ahead, the shoreline resolved into view, a strand of black stones and twisted trees whose branches curled like grasping hands. The colors here seemed wrong, inverted: grass gleamed in bruised blue, and the trees shimmered in hues of ash and bone.

Breasal stirred behind her, the faintest vibration running along his harp strings though no hand touched them. He said nothing. Words here would shatter more than silence.

The boat scraped softly against the shore. Mist clung to the hull, reluctant to release them. Ríona stood first, feeling the Heartstone hum louder with every breath of this broken land.

The stones beneath her boots were slick with sorrow. Every step forward pressed her deeper into the threshold between worlds, between what was and what must be.

Breasal followed silently. His face was drawn, pale beneath the weight of what he could already sense.

***

Behind them, Eolan remained in the boat, a shadow draped in mist. He made no move to follow.

The mist thickened suddenly, swirling at her feet like a tide reconsidering its retreat. Ríona paused, not in hesitation, but in acknowledgement, of the moment, of the cost.

She let her eyes trace the path ahead, then behind.

There was no sound but the soft settling of mist and memory. Even the river held its breath.

For the span of a few heartbeats, she imagined what it might feel like to turn, to speak one last word, to draw Eolan forward or release Breasal's burden with a glance. But the time for gestures had passed. The silence now was sacred.

The path before her did not welcome comfort.

It demanded resolve.

Ríona did not look back.

The wind did not stir.

But something within her did, soft as a memory, sharp as a vow.

She stepped forward, not knowing if the land would answer.

The trees loomed before them, their trunks gnarled by grief, their leaves whispering old songs too fractured to name. Beyond the forest, deeper in the heart of the island, something pulsed in time with the Heartstone, a summons, a reckoning.

Without speaking, Ríona stepped forward into the gloom. Each footfall pulled the mist aside like a curtain, revealing a path only she could walk.

The final trial awaited.

And she would meet it alone.

The silver light ahead brightened as Ríona approached, coalescing into an arch of woven branches and ancient stone. It shimmered not with warmth but with a cold invitation, a summons into herself.

She stepped through without hesitation.

The world shifted.

Gone were the twisted woods and the mourning mist. Instead, she stood in the great hall of Brugh na Bóinne but altered, a hollow echo of home. The sacred fires guttered low. Dust covered the once-proud stones. No crows cried from the rafters. Silence rotted the air.

Before she stood by herself.

***

Not as she was, but as she might have been.

This Ríona wore simple robes faded by time. Her hair was streaked early with gray. Her shoulders were bowed, her hands calloused from tending fields instead of rites. Her eyes, once burning with purpose, were dulled to ash.

The Heartstone was nowhere to be seen. The Morrígan's mark on her spirit was faint as if forgotten as if never called upon.

The other Ríona moved stiffly, tending to a brazier that barely smoldered. She hummed a tune that Ríona half-remembered from childhood, a song of dusk and dying embers.

A voice, her own, yet not her own, whispered from the shadows:

"This could have been yours. A life untouched by burden. A life is safe. A life small."

Ríona's hands trembled at her sides. The weight of it was almost worse than the trials she had faced in the flesh. This was the trial of spirit, of choice.

She stepped closer.

The false Ríona looked up. Their eyes met, not in recognition but in weary acceptance.

Without words, she offered a hand.

An invitation to lay down the Heartstone. To abandon the path of the gods. Returning to the comforts of mortality, forgettable days, and unshaken nights.

Ríona's fingers brushed the Heartstone on her chest. It throbbed once, sharp and painful, reminding her of every sacrifice she had made to reach this moment.

She closed her eyes.

And when she opened them, she stepped back from the offered hand.

The false Ríona smiled, not in anger, sorrow, or fading.

She dissolved into mist, leaving only the echo of that lullaby lost in the still air.

***

The hall cracked apart, and the mist of the actual world rushed in.

Ríona stood alone once more, stronger.

Ahead, beyond the shattered threshold, the final passage awaited.

The mist thickened as Ríona crossed the threshold of twisted trees. The air itself seemed weighted, dense with memory and sorrow. Each step felt like sinking through the layers of forgotten time.

***

Figures began to emerge from the swirling gloom, translucent shapes at first, then more solid, though their edges blurred and wavered. They formed a slow, solemn procession across her path.

Ancient druids in tattered robes, their staves worn smooth by the hands of centuries. Warrior-kings with shattered crowns and shields buckled over time. Women crowned in leaves, cradling the last embers of once-sacred fires.

And among them, taller shadows moved, the gods themselves or what remained of them.

The Dagda, his great club, trailed mist behind him.

148

Brigid, her hair a crown of embers.

Lugh, bearing a light spear, now dimmed to a muted glow.

They passed before her in silence, their eyes hollow, their forms weighed down by the gravity of their own fading.

Breasal played a single, steady note on his harp, a tone so low it barely brushed the air, but it kept the mist from clutching at them.

Ríona bowed her head slightly in respect as each spirit passed. She dared not reach out. Even a single touch might shatter what fragile boundaries still held.

Eolan's presence flickered behind her, distant, more shadow than man. He, too, watched but did not move.

The spirits whispered as they passed, not in words she could understand, but in memories, in ancient griefs, songs of battles lost, oaths broken, blessings forgotten.

The final figure to emerge was a woman in a cloak of crow-feathers, her face hidden beneath a bone mask.

Ríona's breath caught.

The Morrígan.

Or the memory of her.

The crow-queen raised a hand, not in blessing, but in acknowledgment. A farewell.

***

The procession wound onward into the mist, leaving only silence in its wake.

And ahead, where the trees broke apart, a faint silver light shone, the gateway to the heart of the trial.

Ríona steadied her breath, feeling the Heartstone's pulse align with the unseen rhythm beyond.

She stepped forward once more, alone among the fading echoes of gods.

The mist grew thinner, but the weight upon Ríona's spirit deepened.

***

Ahead, a narrow path wound between towering stones inscribed with symbols she could no longer read, forgotten names, severed oaths. The Heartstone beat like a second heart against her chest, urgent and sorrowful.

An altar of black stone stood at the path's center, and upon it, nothing.

Not a relic.

Not a sword.

Only memory.

The mist twisted and coalesced before her, forming shapes drawn from her own soul. She saw Eolan, not as he was now, but as he had been in the first glimmers of loyalty: standing guard beneath the hawthorn tree, his silent vow bright as morning.

She saw her mother, her hands weaving songs through the air, her eyes shining with quiet pride.

She saw herself, laughing once, weeping once, daring once.

Each memory hovered before her like a thread of spun gold, offered in trembling temptation.

A voice rose from the altar, low, patient, merciless:

"To carry the Heartstone forward, you must unmake what binds you."

Ríona's throat tightened. These were not burdens to her, they were her very blood.

But she understood now.

The Heartstone was not a weapon nor a crown. It was a mirror.

And mirrors shattered those who clung to past reflections.

Ríona stepped forward, trembling, and placed her palm upon the stone.

One by one, the memories burned.

The laughter. The vows. The faces.

Not erased. Transformed.

150

Their warmth folded into her chest, no longer separate from her spirit but woven into its root. Not lost, made into something changeless.

(♪ Song: "What the Flame Remembers", see Appendix I)

***

The Heartstone flared once, a searing light that painted the mist with the colors of mourning and dawn.

When the brilliance faded, Ríona stood alone.

Her cloak was tattered. Her eyes were clear. The Heartstone no longer throbbed against her, it pulsed within her.

She had severed the last chain.

And she was ready.

Ahead, through the sundered mist, the actual shrine awaited.

The mist parted at last, revealing a clearing lit by no sun.

The shrine rose at its center, not built, but grown from the bones of the land. Stones twisted upward like the ribs of a sleeping giant, encircling a hollow at their heart.

The Heartstone pulsed once against Ríona's chest, no longer a relic separate from her spirit but a living thread of what she had become.

Breasal approached from the edge of the clearing. His harp was silent now, his face solemn. He did not speak. No words left could cross the distance Ríona had traveled within herself.

Eolan remained behind, a fading shadow among the mist.

Ríona stepped into the center of the shrine.

The earth recognized her. The stones bowed inward, singing without sound.

She knelt, placing her palm against the altar stone grown from the world's first breath.

***

The Heartstone's light bled outward, soaking into the altar, into the roots below, and into the island's veins.

This was not coronation. It was continuity — a vow carried not by priestess or goddess alone, but by the land itself.

The shrine shivered, not in collapse, but in rebirth.

Above, the sky cracked open to reveal a deep violet twilight, and a single crow wheeled high overhead, its cry swallowed by the new stillness.

Ríona rose slowly.

Not as the priestess who had set out.

Not as the girl who had dreamt of prophecy.

But as something new.

Something born of sorrow, silence, and flame.

She turned back to Breasal, her voice steady in the hush:

"It is done."

And together, without ceremony or triumph, they walked from the shrine into the new night, toward the next sorrow, the next hope, the next song.

.

CHAPTER 16
The Choice of Silence

T he hollow beneath her hands was colder than stone. It throbbed faintly, a slow pulse that matched neither her heartbeat nor the earth's rhythm. It was the cadence of something older, an ancient hunger that demanded not blood nor bone but *essence*.

Ríona's fingers trembled.

The mist tightened around the grove, thick as woven cloth. Sounds shrank to nothing. Even her own breath seemed swallowed by the air.

She was alone here.

Not abandoned, *witnessed*. The crow. The Silent Warrior. The memory of her mother braided through the hush.

They watched, but they could not choose.

Only she could open the path.

And the price...

A voice for a vision.

A cry for a flame.

A name for a future not yet born.

Her thoughts swirled like dry leaves:

Without a voice, how would she sing the names of the dead? How would she shape chants to guide the newborn? How would she speak love, anger, grief?

The power she would gain was terrible and bright: the full sight of the Otherworld, unfiltered by the clumsiness of words. But in exchange, she would become a creature of gestures, silence, and unspoken songs.

No spell of healing could restore what she gave.

No prayer could summon it back.

It would be an exile from a part of herself, as profound as stepping beyond the veil.

She gripped the edge of the altar to steady herself.

And in the pause, in the ache of hesitation, came another memory:

A cradle of firelight. Her mother's voice: soft, rough, worn by sorrow. *"You will walk where even I cannot follow. And when you reach that place, remember, the gods do not speak in words. They speak in rivers. In roots. In the ash left after the burning."*

Her voice had always been a gift.

***

But it had never been *hers* to keep.

It had been a bridge. And now, it must become a sacrifice.

Tears spilled unchecked down her cheeks. She let them fall. They sizzled into mist before they reached the ground.

Above, the crow shifted its weight. The Silent Warrior's shadow leaned closer, though he did not touch her. The altar's pulse deepened, a heartbeat beneath the world.

Ríona closed her eyes.

"I was born from breath and flame," she whispered, the last words she would ever utter aloud. "Let me return not as sound but as fire remembered."

And with that vow, she offered herself fully.

She leaned down.

154

And touched her lips to the stone.

The choice was made.

The silence rushed in.

But it was not empty.

It was vast.

It was sacred.

It was hers.

The stone tasted of iron and ash.

When Ríona's lips brushed its surface, the altar stirred beneath her, exhaling a breath of frost that pulled every sound from the grove. Her ears rang with the sudden pressure, but she did not flinch. She kept her mouth pressed against the ancient glyph, sealing her vow.

The ground beneath her knees thrummed. It was a low vibration, slow and inevitable, like the turning of unseen gears deep within the world's marrow.

The mist gathered close.

Above her, the trees bent inward, forming a cathedral of bone and shadow.

The crow cried once, but no sound reached her.

***

The altar responded in kind. A filament of red light traced up from the hollow. It spiraled around Ríona's throat, feather-light, terrible in its gentleness. It tightened, not with pain, but with certainty. A weaving.

The language of the sacrifice unfolded itself in the air:

Not punishment. Not curse.

Transformation.

The glyphs carved into the altar pulsed with an ancient cadence. Spirals ignited in a dull ember glow and dimmed. Ríona's breath grew heavy.

She felt her voice, her *voice*, unravel from her body, pulled not by violence but by invitation.

The first thread of it rose like smoke from her lips. It shimmered in the still air, golden, trembling, before dissolving into the stone.

With each beat of the altar's unseen heart, more threads lifted from her: the memory of her first chant sung beneath the cairn, the lullabies whispered by her mother by firelight, the cries of battle and mourning she had woven into rites.

Each syllable, each note of life she had ever given voice to, was unwound and drawn away.

Yet she felt no pain.

Only...a stretching.

A widening.

As though she were being poured into a vessel too large for her body, a shape too vast for mere words.

Her arms sagged; her head bowed.

The Silent Warrior knelt beside her, silent witness to the last moments of the voice he had once guarded.

The crow descended from its perch atop the leaning stone and landed near the altar, wings slightly unfurled. Its gaze pinned her, ancient, merciless, tender.

A final gust of wind passed through the clearing, stirring the mist into spirals.

And then,

Stillness.

The threads of Ríona's voice, invisible now, had all been gathered.

***

The altar's hollow closed like the sealing of a wound.

The mist thinned.

The weight in her chest lessened, leaving a strange clarity in its place.

Nothing came when she tried to speak, to offer a prayer, a cry, even a name.

Not even a whisper.

The world did not mourn the loss.

It bent to it.

The trees straightened, their hollow trunks shivering once.

The altar's stones sank slightly into the earth as if exhaling.

The crow dipped its head low as if bowing not in pity but in recognition.

***

And within the vault of Ríona's silence bloomed a new sight:

The threads of life and death weave the land.

The spirits slumbering at the roots.

The gods watching from the edges of the world, veiled but awake.

She had crossed the threshold, not by sword or chant, but by sacrifice.

Ríona rose, her knees unsteady but her spirit unbroken.

The path forward had opened.

And though no word would ever leave her lips again, the world had begun to speak to her in the tongue of flame, stone, and wing.

She stepped away from the altar.

And did not look back.

The grove no longer pulsed with threat.

It breathed with her now.

Every stone, every broken tree, every fragment of mist felt stitched into her skin, as though the price she had paid was not the loss of her voice but the sealing of her spirit into the land's memory.

Ríona moved carefully across the clearing, her footsteps soundless even to herself. She could feel the earth's vibrations as clearly as heartbeat and breath: the shudder of stones grieving their erosion, the sigh of ancient roots tangled far below.

Her throat ached, not with pain, but with *absence*, like a hollow space carved too precisely to ever heal.

The Silent Warrior followed at a respectable distance, his gaze sharper than before, almost wary, as if he sensed the shift in her silence and being.

She paused before the altar's edge, glancing again at the hollow that had taken her last words. It gleamed faintly, a dim spiral of red slowly fading into darkness.

There would be no reclaiming what she had given.

***

But in the vacancy left behind, something new had rooted itself.

She raised her hand, feeling the tendrils of the Otherworld curling at the edges of her perception. Not visions. Not dreams. Truths. Unfiltered, raw, waiting only to be noticed.

The crow alighted on her shoulder without ceremony, its claws careful against the thick wool of her cloak. It did not caw. It needed no sound.

Ríona turned toward the deeper path that had opened at the grove's far edge, a gap between two leaning stones where none had existed. Beyond it, mist churned against the ground in slow waves, and the faint throb of something powerful, a heartbeat older than gods, beckoned.

The Heartstone was nearby.

Her hand brushed the hilt of her blade out of habit, though she knew instinctively that no weapon of iron or flesh would serve her now. She would face what lay ahead not with voice, not steel, but with memory sharpened into will.

She glanced once at the Silent Warrior.

He inclined his head, a silent question.

Are you ready?

She answered without words, stepping forward, her shadow stretched long behind her.

***

The mist folded around them, the crow whispering only in the language of shifting feathers and steady weight.

The clearing faded away.

The shattered grove, the altar, the trees bent to her silence, all fell behind like a chapter finished and sealed.

Ahead, the veil between worlds thinned to the width of a breath.

And Ríona, no longer merely the priestess of The Morrígan but something more, something shaped by vow and sacrifice, walked into the mist, unafraid.

The earth remembered her now.

And the gods were beginning to stir.

CHAPTER 17

THE HEARTSTONE REVEALED

T he mist thinned as they walked, peeling away from the stones like torn fabric.

***

Ahead, the land sloped downward, folding into a hollow encircled by ancient black stones. No hand had placed them, they had risen, it seemed, at the command of something deep beneath the earth, thrust upward in defiance or sorrow.

Ríona moved silently, the crow a dark weight upon her shoulder. The Silent Warrior matched her steps with tireless patience. The world's breath grew colder as they descended, each step sinking into a loam that seemed to hum with memory.

The hollow was a wound in the landscape, a bowl carved by time and grief. Within it, the Heartstone pulsed, not a stone at all, but something more: a vast shard of translucent crystal, veined with fire and mist, rising from the earth like the broken tooth of a fallen god.

The Heartstone sang without sound.

Its song braided itself into Ríona's bones, threading through the empty space where her voice had once lived. It was a music of becoming and unbecoming, of gods who had risen and fallen, of mortal wills sharpening into weapons.

She slowed, each step heavier than the last.

Around the Heartstone, the grass was a sickly silver-green, trembling without a breeze. The stones marking the hollow's rim leaned inward as though pulled by the gravity of the relic's sorrow.

The crow shifted its weight, talons digging gently into Ríona's cloak. Beside her, the Silent Warrior placed a hand over his heart, a gesture of reverence or warning. No barrier blocked their path. No guardian rose. And yet, deep in her marrow, Ríona felt it: this place did not welcome the uninvited. It tolerated them only because it remembered her sacrifice.

The Heartstone flared faintly. Within its crystalline depths flickered not reflections, but memories trapped in glass, battles fought before language, spirits rising from river and stone, the faces of gods who once walked the world unveiled and unafraid. Her hands itched with a hunger she could not name.

***

Without words, she and the Silent Warrior stepped forward. The world narrowed to the pulse of light within the shard. Each beat called to something older than breath, older than the chant-magic that once filled her lungs. Each beat whispered: *Remember. Choose. Wake.*

Ríona reached out, hand trembling with the knowing. The Heartstone was waiting, not to be taken, but to be claimed.

At the hollow's heart, the Heartstone loomed.

It was no mere relic, no polished artifact of mortal hands.

It was a shard of the first dawn, a wound left when the world was young, and the gods danced openly upon the earth.

The Heartstone rose taller than any man, a towering prism of translucent crystal. Beneath its fractured surface, rivers of light and shadow churned, never still, as if entire storms were trapped within its core. The glow was not steady, it flared and ebbed like breathing, like the slow, tidal heart of the earth itself.

Ríona stepped closer, and the mist peeled back fully, reluctantly, like a curtain torn from sacred mysteries. The stone's surface shimmered between states, now clear as ice, now dark as storm clouds.

Shapes stirred within: stags crowned with woven boughs, rivers spilling silver through blackened fields, the blood of forgotten kings mingling with the roots of ancient trees.

It was not memory.

It was *becoming*.

This was where stories broke and mended; blood, song, and stone were bound into one long, aching weave.

The Silent Warrior stayed at the hollow's rim, half-shrouded by mist.

He knew, as she knew, that this was not his threshold to cross.

The crow abandoned her shoulder, circling once before alighting atop a leaning stone.

It cawed once, a rough, broken note, but no sound reached Ríona's ears.

It was not needed.

The Heartstone's song was already inside her.

It pulled at the threads of her spirit, seeking the patterns woven into her silence and sacrifice. It did not call for dominance or conquest, it called for remembrance and acceptance, for surrender to the truth of all things:

That no god remained unchanged.

That no mortal held dominion forever.

All things must pass through fire, silence, and forgetting and be reborn.

Her knees weakened, but she did not fall. She stepped closer until her reflection caught in the Heartstone's surface, yet it was not only her face she saw.

Within her gaze bloomed visions: The Morrígan's wings eclipsing a burning field. The Dagda's great staff, broke and mended anew. Danu's river hands cradling both life and ruin.

The Heartstone pulsed again, and Ríona's spirit flinched beneath the enormity of it. This was no reward, no triumph, only the crushing gravity of history pressing against her as the stones of Newgrange pressed upon the bones of the dead.

And still, she reached out.

Not for glory, not for prophecy, but for the pulse of a promise whispered long ago beneath the sacred dark of Brugh na Bóinne: *Let me be a flame that remembers when others forget.*

Her hand hovered inches from the Heartstone's surface.

***

True vision was coming, and the price, like every price, would leave its mark.

The moment Ríona's fingertips grazed the Heartstone, the world shattered, with sound or violence, with revelation.

***

The hollow, the stones, the Silent Warrior, all fell away, peeled back like thin bark to reveal a sky of seething, molten memory. She stood no longer on soil but upon a vast expanse of woven light, threads trembling with the breath of gods and mortals alike.

The Heartstone flared, and her spirit was pulled inward.

She plunged through rivers of time, visions flaring in flashes too swift to hold. The Morrígan stood alone on a battlefield of crows and blood, her eyes black as the space between stars. The Dagda's great cauldron overturned, spilling its unending bounty into cracked, thirsty fields. Brigid wept fire over a broken loom, its threads of inspiration snapping to ash. Lugh knelt before a flame he could not quench, his spear abandoned at his feet.

The gods were not falling, they were fading.

Once rooted in the marrow of the world, their essence shriveled beneath the weight of mortal forgetting. Each unsung

164

song, each broken oath, each shrine left to ruin severed another thread. The weave frayed before her eyes.

In its place, new threads spun, sharp, thin, restless. Mortals rose. Kings crowned themselves not by divine blessing, but by sword and coin. Druids twisted into warlords. Priestesses became relics.

She saw the land fracture: rivers turned to dust, forests blackened, stones split as the sacred flows withered.

And from the dark beyond the weave, something stirred, faceless, nameless, hunger given shape. Not born of the gods. Not born of man. But waiting to devour what both had forsaken.

The Heartstone pulsed again, harder. Ríona staggered under the weight of the visions, her spirit stretched thin. But deeper still, beneath ruin and sorrow, she glimpsed something else: a silver thread winding through a broken loom, a single crow feather falling into flame, not consumed, but transformed, and a woman standing between worlds, neither goddess nor mortal, bearing the weight of both. A bridge. A guardian.

Not to restore the old ways, but to birth something new from the ashes. The Heartstone trembled. It did not command. It offered.

Ríona understood she was not meant to save the past. She was meant to carry it forward, to let it shape her, but not bind her. To become a memory walking, a silence that spoke, a flame that would not die.

This was not sacrifice for power — it was sacrifice for continuity. A vow that memory, even when buried, must still be carried.

The vision tore at its edges. Threads of futures unraveled, pulling her backward. She gasped, soundless.

And in that final flicker of light, one last image seared into her soul: the Heartstone shattering, and a shadowed hand reaching for the pieces. Not hers. Another's. Already moving. Already coming. The light collapsed inward like breath.

***

Ríona staggered, hand braced against the mist-slick ground. Her chest ached with a hollow pain, as if the visions had carved rooms inside her no memory could fill.

She had walked through fire and silence alike.

Now even the silence knew her name.

Before her, the Heartstone pulsed, slow, steady, waiting. It had shown her gods fading, futures fraying, hunger growing. But it had not commanded her. The choice was hers.

The crow flapped once, sending a soundless wind across the hollow. The Silent Warrior waited beyond the stones. Ríona rose. Trembling, but steady. She stepped forward. The Heartstone shimmered. Reflections danced across its face, druids, queens, nameless poets who had sung the world awake and wept it to sleep.

She was not the first to stand here. But she would be the last.

***

Her hand hovered over its surface. The air crackled with unseen threads. Not a relic to take. A covenant to seal. Ríona pressed her palm to the Heartstone. For a breath, nothing moved. Then it blazed.

Not blinding, revealing. The old songs spiraled into her. The wars. The weeping. The gods forgotten. She tasted iron. She heard lullabies buried beneath oceans. The stone spoke no words. It became part of her.

Her silence deepened, not as absence, but as power. Silver and crimson threads curled up her arms, glyphs only spirits would see. Not marks of ownership, vows. The light dimmed. She pulled her hand away. But the bond remained.

The Heartstone no longer sang alone. It sang through her. And she, once priestess, was now a bearer of broken futures and a guardian of remembering flame.

Mist stirred at her feet. Far away, something felt the Heartstone's choice. Something shifted. Something woke. Ríona turned from the stone, fear striking her chest, not panic, but clarity. The gods would not stop what was coming. Neither could she. But she could stand between. And she could endure.

***

The mist changed, colder now, sharper, moving with intent. The Silent Warrior tensed. The crow rose, wings wide. Ríona felt it too. The stir. The awakening. Something had waited behind the veil. Not a god. Not a mortal. Something older.

A presence fed not by worship, but by forgetting. She pressed her hand to her chest. The Heartstone's rhythm beat within her. It shielded her, but it also marked her. In the mist, shapes began to move. She could not see them, but she felt their hunger.

They were waiting, not for the stone, but for her. The crow dipped, brushing her hair. The Silent Warrior signaled: move. Ríona did not run. She walked. She was the bridge now. And bridges do not flee. They hold.

She turned from the hollow, into the path the world had opened. The Silent Warrior followed, blade half-drawn. The sky held its breath. The crow veered west, toward the thinning veil. Toward what waited next.

Ríona didn't look back. She didn't need to. The Heartstone was within her now, a shard of fire, a vow etched in bone. Behind her, in the mist-wracked hollow, something vast stirred fully awake. And followed.

CHAPTER 18

PURSUIT

The mist swallowed the hollow behind them.

No cries rang out.

No horns sounded.

And yet Ríona knew with a certainty beyond sight or sound:
They were being hunted.

The Silent Warrior moved at her side; his blade half-bared.
The crow circled once overhead, wings carving silent arcs through
the thickening air.

***

Once faintly marked by leaning stones and forgotten shrines, the
path westward had become a maze of broken ground and
shadowed thickets. Roots snaked over the earth like veins, slick
and cold. The sky above sagged heavily and colorless, pressing
down until every breath felt borrowed.

Ríona pressed a hand against the Heartstone's thrum in her
chest.

It beat faster now, not with panic, but with warning.

Behind them, the mist thickened unnaturally. Shapes moved
within it, slow at first, like half-born thoughts, but sharpening with
each breath she took.

Not men.

Not beasts.

Something between.

The Hollowed had come awake.

***

Creatures of memory's forgetting, echoes twisted by ages of neglect, hunger born from the slow death of stories left untold. They moved without feet, without faces, their forms blurring and snapping with each broken memory they devoured.

Ríona tightened her cloak around her shoulders and pressed forward faster now.

The Silent Warrior matched her pace without the need for words.

There was no defense here, no sanctuary to be found.

Only flight.

And still the mist deepened, as if the land itself wished to forget its own breath.

No mercy waited, only the shape of the unknown.

The crow darted ahead, a black arrow cutting through the mist, and Ríona followed, feet slipping on wet stone, heart hammering a rhythm that was not fear but fierce, silent defiance.

The mist curled tighter around their path, pressing into her skin like cold hands.

And still, the Hollowed came.

Not with roars.

Not with howls.

With silence more profound than hers.

A silence that is unmade.

They fled into the broken vale ahead, where rivers once braided through sacred fields, now choked with ash and bone.

Where the old protections are no longer held.

Where memory alone could not shield them.

Ríona dared a glance back once, only once, and saw them:

Tall and thin, stitched from scraps of form and forgetting, with hollow spaces where faces might have been.

They moved without effort, without haste, and patient as tide and ruin.

She turned her gaze forward and ran harder, the weight of the Heartstone burning against her chest.

The gods had faded.

The veil had thinned.

And now the things that fed on forgetting had come to claim the remnants of a broken world.

Unless she reached the next threshold.

Unless she endured.

The mist behind them thickened until it was no longer mist but a wall, a living, breathing thing pressing forward with dreadful intent.

Ríona did not look back.

She didn't need to.

She felt them, just beyond the reach of sight, the Hollowed, the Forgotten, the Nameless Ones, closing the distance with each heartbeat. They moved like memory unraveling, silent but swift, weaving between broken stones and bent trees with a hunger sharpened by centuries of waiting.

The Silent Warrior signaled with a sharp tilt of his head: faster.

Ríona nodded once, gathering her cloak closer as they fled down the crumbling path, their feet scattering stones worn smooth by long-forgotten pilgrimages.

The crow shrieked overhead, a dry, broken sound like a blade scraping stone, before veering sharply westward.

Follow.

Trust.

The ground sloped unevenly, fractured by time and old rites left to rot. What was once sacred was now dangerous, hollows in the earth, roots reaching like skeletal fingers, slick moss hiding unseen chasms.

A place meant to slow the unwelcome.

A place that remembered betrayal.

Behind them, the Hollowed moved faster.

Their forms were half-made, like statues chiseled by blind hands, elongated limbs, eyeless faces, mouths that opened but uttered no sound. They loped forward with inhuman grace, undeterred by obstacles that would have crippled mortal feet.

They did not tire.

They did not doubt.

They came.

Ríona stumbled once, her boot catching on an unseen snag, and the mist clawed at her back for a heartbeat, cold as a forgotten grave. But the Silent Warrior caught her elbow, steadying her without breaking stride.

Ahead, the crow dove low, disappearing into a cleft between two ancient stones, a threshold barely wide enough for them to pass.

A narrowing.

A choice.

Ríona plunged after it without hesitation, her body folding through the jagged gap. The Silent Warrior slipped behind her, the mist biting at their heels.

The Hollowed hesitated.

Ríona felt a brief, confused pause as if the threshold resisted them, not entirely barring their way but slowing them, pressing against their forms like a half-remembered barrier.

It would not hold long.

Nothing truly forgotten could be forbidden forever.

They ran into a new clearing, but the air was wrong even here.

Stale.

Charged.

The land ahead fractured into a labyrinth of fallen standing stones and brackish pools reflecting a sky that no longer remembered the sun.

The Heartstone throbbed once beneath Ríona's skin.

Warning.

The pursuit was not over.

It had only just begun.

The clearing opened into a wasteland.

Where once sacred streams had wound through lush groves, now only brackish pools remained, their surfaces filmed with the gray scum of abandonment. Fallen stones jutted like broken teeth from cracked earth, their carvings eroded by centuries of forgotten prayers.

The air tasted wrong here, stale, sour, heavy with the memory of unfinished rites.

Ríona hesitated at the threshold, not out of fear of the Hollowed, whose shapes were still twisted in the mist behind, but from a deeper instinct.

The land itself recoiled from their presence.

The crow swooped low, calling a sound like splintered wood once before veering sharply across the shattered field.

No safe path marked the way.

No guiding stones remained upright.

Only ruin and risk.

The Silent Warrior glanced to Ríona, awaiting her lead.

She felt the pull of the Heartstone within her chest, a rhythm now steady and grim. It did not urge her forward nor hold her back.

It bore witness.

This was not a path chosen for her.

This was a path she must choose.

Ríona stepped forward, boots splashing through the shallow muck. The ground sucked at her steps, reluctant to release her as if the land itself mourned what it had become.

The Silent Warrior followed the blade drawn but held low, not against enemies of flesh, but against the despair that oozed from the broken vale like mist from an open wound.

Each step deeper into the field pulled at her spirit.

Whispers stirred at the edges of her hearing, not from the Hollowed behind, but from the stones themselves:

Why walk where gods have fallen?

Why carry memory into a world that has already been forgotten?

Ríona pressed onward, her silence a shield against the creeping voices.

Each breath burned.

Each heartbeat echoed against the broken bones of the earth.

The Hollowed reached the vale's edge.

There, they faltered.

The ground resisted them, not entirely, but enough.

Their blurred forms wavered, flickering in and out of shape as they struggled to cross the threshold into sacred ruin.

***

The land, though broken, still remembered its purpose. It couldn't bar the Hollowed forever, but it could slow them. Buy moments.

Ríona quickened her pace, skirting black pools that shimmered with false visions: her mother weeping blood, the crow ablaze, the Heartstone shattered and lost. Lies, born of grief.

The Silent Warrior grunted, stumbling as a sunken stone shifted beneath him.

He righted himself with a sharp jerk of his arm and pressed on.

There was no safety in standing still, only in reaching the far side, where the mist thinned, where memory and forgetting no longer battled in every breath.

***

Ahead, a broken archway loomed at the vale's far end, the last remnant of an ancient passage once used by those who had dared to walk between worlds.

The crow circled above, crying out with urgency.

Ríona fixed her gaze on the crumbling arch, not salvation, not sanctuary, only a way forward. She did not run. She endured. One step. Another. Each breath heavier than the last, each heartbeat threading her closer to the threshold.

Behind them, the Hollowed howled without mouths, their rage and hunger mounting. The broken vale shuddered beneath their feet, and the chase entered its final phase.

The archway loomed, broken, crumbling, half-swallowed by mist. It was no grand gate. No threshold shining.

Only two leaning stones and a shattered lintel, etched with symbols so weathered they barely clung to meaning.

Yet even in ruin, the passage remembered its purpose.

It would mark a crossing.

A severance.

(♪ Song: "Blood on the Threshold", see Appendix I)

Ríona pushed forward, boots sinking into the sodden earth. The crow swooped ahead, a black blur against the dimness. The Silent Warrior stayed close at her side, his breath ragged but steady, his blade still drawn though it would do little against what hunted them.

The Hollowed surged behind, not sprinting, not leaping, but gliding as if propelled by the tide of forgetting itself.

They would not falter again.

The broken vale had slowed them.

But here, at the crumbling arch, they would press through.

Ríona tightened her grip on the satchel that carried the Heartstone's resonance, feeling the heavy thrum of its memory against her ribs.

The choice sharpened in her mind: cross and be wounded, stay and be unmade. There was no perfect path, only cost.

***

The crow screamed once, high and piercing, and veered through the archway without hesitation. Ríona ran after it, feet splashing through a shallow pool that reflected nothing of her but shadow and flame.

At the threshold, the mist clawed at her, thick and cold as iron chains. Her body strained forward, but something caught.

The Heartstone.

Its bond still tied her to the land behind. The hollow's memory clung to her spirit.

She wasn't merely crossing into another place; she was breaking a tie.

The stones of the arch hummed sharply, a vibration that shot up her bones and lanced through the markings invisibly etched upon her skin.

She gasped, clutching her chest as the searing pain blossomed.

Behind, the Silent Warrior thrust her forward, his strength driving her through the resistance.

The mist shrieked, a soundless rending.

Something within her tore free.

Not the Heartstone itself, that bond held.

But part of her memory, her sense of belonging to the sacred hollow, snapped like a string stretched too far.

***

Ríona stumbled across the threshold, falling hard onto the ash-strewn ground beyond.

The Silent Warrior followed, his cloak torn, his blade dripping not blood but something darker, the smear of broken memory itself.

***

The Hollowed surged to the arch and recoiled.

The ancient passage shuddered, the air around it warping with unseen force.

The Hollowed paced beyond it, circling, clawing at the mists that bled from the broken stones, but they did not cross.

Not yet.

Not here.

The Silent Warrior offered Ríona his hand, pulling her to her feet without a word.

She stood trembling, not from exhaustion or fear, but from the aching hole now carved within her spirit.

The cost had been paid.

A part of her was left behind, cradled by the broken vale.

She would not be able to call upon it again.

No returning.

No mending.

Only forward now.

The crow circled overhead, a silent guardian against a sky that remembered neither sun nor stars.

Ríona pressed her palm against her heart, feeling the diminished but steady pulse of the Heartstone within her.

The world had changed.

And so did she.

They turned westward, toward the place where the veil thinned to almost nothing and began to walk.

***

Behind them, the Hollowed howled once, long and low, the soundless echo of hunger denied.

ACT III

The Flame That Remembers

To return is not to go back.

It is to carry the silence forward, and make it sing.

CHAPTER 19

THE MORRÍGAN'S EMBRACE

They crossed into twilight.

The mist had thinned, but the air remained heavy, soaked with the weight of unseen eyes. The earth beneath their feet shifted, no longer resisting but offering little strength to their steps. Each pace forward carved more from Ríona's spirit.

***

Her body rebelled when they reached the low hill crowned by a broken thorn tree. Her knees buckled. She collapsed, her palms scraping across gravel and root.

The Silent Warrior knelt beside her at once, but she waved him back weakly, her breath ragged, her limbs trembling as if hollowed out from within.

The crow circled once above them, a black spiral against the dimming sky, then landed heavily on a nearby stone. It watched, silent, waiting.

Waiting.

Ríona pressed a hand against her chest, against the slow pulse of the Heartstone's binding. It beat still, steady, relentless, but it no longer answered her commands. It now throbbed with its own will, braided into something older and darker than her name.

She shuddered. The weight of memory, promise, and sacrifice bore down until even thought unraveled.

And in that unraveling, she heard the wings. Not the crow's. Greater wings. Wings woven of storm and blood and mourning songs lost to human tongues.

The Morrígan.

***

She came not as a vision, not as a dream. She came as the storm, tearing through the veil between worlds, spilling across the broken hill like a tide of black feathers and steel-gray mist.

The Silent Warrior recoiled, lowering his head in reverence, or fear.

The crow flared its wings wide and cried out once, a sharp, guttural note that split the heavy air.

Ríona could not rise. She could only lift her gaze through the shaking of her body, through the burning in her veins, to behold the shape of her goddess.

The Morrígan stood before her, shifting, mercurial, terrible. One moment, a woman crowned in antlered shadows. The next, a crow with eyes like molten iron. The next, a battlefield strewn with broken oaths and blood-soaked banners. She was not singular. She was not bound by form. She was war, remembrance, and death made a memory. And she had come for Ríona.

Ríona bowed her head until her forehead touched the soil, surrendering not out of fear but out of knowing: she had given voice, had given memory, had borne silence. Now, she would give herself. Not servant. Not priestess. Something more.

The Morrígan spoke without sound, her voice shaping itself in the marrow of Ríona's bones:

"You are hollowed by vow. You are forged by silence. You are mine."

The earth trembled beneath her. The roots of the thorn tree shivered, shedding dry leaves like brittle prayers.

182

Ríona's heart did not resist. It opened. And in that opening, the goddess poured herself like molten iron into the flesh and spirit of the waiting vessel.

The world dimmed. Ríona gasped, but no voice rose.

Only breath. Only blood. Only a new, terrible song threading itself into the hollows of her being. She was falling. She was flying. She was becoming.

***

The world unstitched itself. Not torn, not shattered, but unspooled like a thread from a loom no longer tended.

Ríona rose without rising. Her body, her bones, the very marrow of her being remained knelt upon the broken hill. But her spirit, fierce and fragile, soared. Wings she did not possess carried her upward, borne on the black storm that was the Morrígan's breath.

Mist and stone fell away beneath her. The world blurred into rivers of memory and ruin. Above her, the sky cracked open, a dome of bruised violet and gold.

And The Morrígan flew. Not as a single crow, but as a thousand, a legion, a tide of black wings and iron beaks. A flock vast enough to blot the stars. A shadow stretching from horizon to horizon.

***

Ríona flew within it, part of it, her silence a song woven into the greater scream of unseen winds.

Below, the land burned and bled. Fields once sacred were now stripped bare; their rivers turned to red clay and smoke. Villages huddled beneath broken stones; their people crouched over fires that gave no warmth. Priestesses stood alone in crumbling circles, their chants thin and dying in the air. She saw kings crowned with iron and fear, not wisdom. Druids twisted by ambition, hoarding knowledge like hoarded gold. Temples to forgotten gods collapsing into the same dust as the altars of men.

The Morrígan's voice thrummed through the flight, not in words, but in pulses of blood and storm:

"This is the path of forgetting. This is the harvest sown by broken oaths. This is the fruit of silence."

Ríona cried out, or tried to, but no sound passed her lips. Only the beat of wings answered. Only the endless surge of dark feathers and broken dreams.

Through the haze, she glimpsed sacred places still standing, faint and far between a lone tree, gnarled and defiant, crowned by a halo of crows. A spring whose waters shimmered silver, untouched by ruin. A single stone cairn, its spiral markings still whispering to the stars.

Hope. Not gone. Not yet. But drowning.

The Morrígan wheeled suddenly, and the entire flock turned with her, an impossible, terrible grace.

Ríona's spirit reeled, dragged along in the vast spiral. They dove, plunging into the heart of a battlefield that was both memory and prophecy.

Warriors clashed beneath them, faceless and countless. Blood slicked the ground until it reflected the wounded sky. Crows feasted on the fallen even as they fell.

***

And at the center, a shadowed figure, half-human, half-hunger, reaching for a broken shard of the Heartstone. The same vision she had seen before. Closer now. More real. More inevitable.

The Morrígan's many voices wrapped around her, a chorus woven of storm and sorrow:

"Witness. Remember. Become."

The flight tore onward through smoke, ruin, and the silence of prayers unanswered. Until there was only Ríona, and the choice yet to come.

The storm of wings slowed. Ríona hovered between worlds, body rooted to the broken hill, spirit still adrift in the Morrígan's dark spiral.

***

The sky above her pulsed like a living wound, stitched with the cries of unseen crows. Within that trembling space, she felt The Morrígan draw near, not as a figure but as a voice, force, and blood recognizing blood.

The goddess did not ask. She waited.

Ríona understood. This was no place for demands, no place for doubt. Only the naked truth of vow.

She had been prepared from the first breath stolen from her mother's lips beneath Newgrange's vaulted stone. She had been prepared when she sang the rites into hollow air. She had been prepared when she gave up her voice and took the Heartstone into herself.

Everything until now had been descent. This was the burning. The shaping. The choosing.

***

Kneeling upon the broken hill in the chill of a forgotten twilight, Ríona pressed her forehead to the earth. And in the silence that rose, vast, weightless, eternal, she spoke without words:

I do not serve. I do not plead. I become.

Her heart surged, and the Heartstone answered, its pulse blending into the deeper rhythm of Morrígan's breath.

The earth beneath her responded. A low, resonant hum throbbed through the stones, through the roots of the thorn tree, through the veins of the crow perched nearby, as if all the world's forgotten places remembered themselves for one breathless moment.

A shudder passed through her, not pain, not fear. Recognition. Acceptance.

She lifted her head and opened her hands, palms skyward. In response, The Morrígan descended. Not as flame. Not as thunder.

***

A flood of crows and storm light poured into Ríona's waiting spirit, weaving into the marrow of her bones. Her skin prickled with unseen markings. Her sight sharpened, layering the living and the dead into one vast tapestry.

She saw rivers winding like veins across a dying land. She saw battlefields yet to be soaked with mortal blood. She saw her face reflected in a hundred songs not yet sung, fierce, shadowed, endless.

***

The Morrígan's final whisper sank into her spine:

"Carry wrath as memory. Carry memory as flame. Carry flame as mercy."

The vow sealed itself without chain, without command. It was a choice. It was becoming. It was the last actual act of her own mortal will.

And in choosing, Ríona ceased to be merely herself. She became a vessel of memory sharpened into blade and wing. A flame that would not falter, even as gods and kings fell to dust.

The darkness that had held her unfurled. Ríona drew a breath, deep, ragged, alive with something more than mortal air. She opened her eyes.

The world had sharpened. Where once mist and twilight dulled the edges of stones and trees, now everything burned with a fierce, uncanny clarity.

She could see the pulse of sap within the twisted thorn tree. She could hear the slow weeping of stones buried deep beneath the soil. She could taste the old names trembling in the wind, names forgotten even by those who had once sung them into being.

She did not speak the names aloud.

She did not need to.

186

The land had already begun to remember.

And in that memory, it wept.

Not with sorrow, but with recognition.

She rose to her feet, slowly, steadily, the earth reluctant to release her as if knowing what she had become.

The Silent Warrior watched from a respectable distance, his sword lowered, his head slightly bowed. He saw it, too. She was not what she had been.

The crow flared its wings and cawed sharply, not in alarm, but in a rough blessing.

Ríona touched her chest, feeling the thrumming bond of the Heartstone still lodged within her spirit, but now braided with another heartbeat, older and wilder: The Morrígan's.

Her hands bore faint marks now, glyphs written not in ink but in the memory of storm and blood. Spirals, feathers, rivers twisting into runes only the dead could thoroughly read.

A dark sheen coiled along her limbs, not armor, not cloth, but a shifting mantle of shadow and wing. It did not weigh her down. It lifted her.

When she moved, the mist recoiled slightly as though recognizing a force it dared not oppose.

She was no longer merely the High Priestess of the Morrígan. She was the flame at the edge of memory. The crow on the battlefield's breath. The silence that bore witness when all songs failed. A bridge between what was dying and what must yet be born.

Without a word, she stepped forward, and the broken hill seemed to steady beneath her weight. The Silent Warrior stepped beside her, offering no question, no command. Only loyalty, fierce and unwavering.

Together, they moved westward toward the thin places where the veil tore like gauze in the winter wind, where battle and betrayal waited unseen.

Each step Ríona took left no mark upon the soil, and yet the land remembered her passing.

Above, the first true crows of the mortal world gathered in the thorn branches, watching her with gleaming eyes. Their cries stitched themselves into the air:

Not mourning. No warning. Naming.

The Morrígan's daughter. Memory's flame. Silent wrath. Keeper of the Broken Song.

Ríona did not flinch. She did not falter. She walked.

The gods would not save this world. The mortals would not save it either. But she would remember. She would bear witness. And where memory failed, she would burn a path through forgetting.

CHAPTER 20

THE BATTLE FOR THE HEARTSTONE

"Some echoes are not meant to fade.
They choose where they dwell."
— *Inscription at the Listening Stone, Mirael*

T he world held its breath.

Ríona stood upon a rise of broken stone, the Heartstone's weight thrumming deep in her spirit. Around her, the mist had receded, revealing the land in stark, colorless relief, a barren field once sacred but now scarred by centuries of forgetting.

The Silent Warrior waited at her side, sword drawn, his stance loose but ready. The crow perched atop the twisted stump of an ancient yew, feathers bristling, its black eyes sharp with knowing.

The ground itself trembled faintly, not from thunder or storm, but from the march of those who had come to claim what she carried. They came from all sides: rogues among the druids, stripped of sacred memory, lusting for the Heartstone's power; mortal warbands, crowned by violence, not rite; and stitched among them, the Hollowed, remnant shades drawn by the scent of memory burning.

***

Ríona's vision sharpened. There were hundreds. Perhaps more. Far more than she and the Silent Warrior could face. But the battle was not of numbers. It never had been.

The Heartstone pulsed harder against her ribs, not with fear, but with recognition. This was the place. This was the hour.

Above, the sky seethed. Clouds spiraled outward like a wound stitched with slow-moving crows. The air thickened with iron and ash.

The enemies formed ragged lines, banners torn, faces hollowed by ambition. Some bore twisted remnants of druidic marks, others nothing but hard stares and empty chants. At their center stood a tall figure cloaked in bone-white cloth, helm fashioned of antlers and broken crow feathers. A corrupted druid lord.

He lifted a staff carved from a dead branch, and the earth groaned in answer.

The crow let out a rattling cry. The Silent Warrior braced himself, his blade gleaming beneath the swirling sky. Ríona stepped forward, silent and steady. Her mantle of shadow and wing flowed without wind.

She felt no fear.

Only the certainty of the storm.

The sky answered with thunder.

Not sound, but memory cracking open.

Each step forward summoned the weight of every vow ever made beneath this sky.

The Heartstone pulsed with the cadence of her breath. Not weapon. Not shield. Memory forged into flame.

***

The enemies roared; a soundless howl caught in the mist and began their advance.

The first wave struck like a broken tide. They came without banners or cries, a surge of blades and hunger. The ground shook beneath them.

The Silent Warrior moved first, blade flashing like cold fire. He fought not with rage, but with ruthless precision.

Ríona followed.

She raised no weapon. She needed none.

The first to reach her swung an axe. She lifted her hand.

The air rippled. The axe faltered. A thousand forgotten battles pressed down.

She brushed his chest. He collapsed; spirit dragged into the earth.

The tide surged. For each foe struck down, three more came. The Silent Warrior carved a path beside her. He blocked a spear meant for her heart.

Ríona advanced, her silence a shield. The land fought beside her, roots snared feet, stones shifted subtly, memory made manifest.

***

From the enemy ranks came twisted druids chanting in broken tongues. Coils of bloody mist thickened, wrapping around her.

The Silent Warrior struck down two. Three more rose.

The crows cried out.

Ríona dropped to one knee, pressed her palm to the earth.

The Heartstone flared. Red spirals of light unfolded from the stones.

The mist hissed. The druids faltered.

She rose, shadow-mantle flaring wide. Fear finally touched her enemies.

The Silent Warrior returned to her side. The enemy regrouped.

The druid lord lifted his staff.

The second wave was coming.

They came faster.

The sky offered no solace, only a weight of ash and memory.

Each footfall echoed louder, not in sound but in cost.

And still she pressed forward, not to win, but to endure.

Harder.

The corrupted druids led them now, their staffs striking the earth and unraveling the wards Ríona had drawn. Mist twisted and thickened.

The Silent Warrior fought but began to falter.

A spear grazed the crow. It shrieked, stayed aloft.

Ríona tightened her stance. The Heartstone strained. Too much memory. Too much loss.

The horned leader raised his staff.

A bolt of sickly green light lanced toward her.

The Silent Warrior was too far. The crow too slow.

Ríona raised her hand.

The bolt struck.

Pain split her. The Heartstone absorbed the blow and cracked.

***

A web of crimson light spread through her soul.

The leader howled. The enemies surged.

The crow spiraled lower, weaving glyphs in the air with its cries.

Ríona rose, staggering. The Heartstone flickered.

She saw the battlefield with Morrígan's eyes: every foe a thread, every chant a blade.

If she fell, memory itself would fall.

She drew a breath.

There was only one path.

She must call the storm.

The first feather fell.

A black ember from the sky.

The Silent Warrior nodded.

The horned leader bellowed.

Ríona lifted her arms.

The sky tore open.

Feathers fell like blades. The ground shuddered.

***

Thousands of crows. Wings beat the sky into a weapon.

She became the Morrígan's storm.

The Crowstorm descended.

Crows tore through magic and flesh alike. The corrupted druids screamed as their chants shattered.

The Silent Warrior surged forward, blade as wrathful as the storm.

The horned leader summoned green fire around him. Ríona turned her gaze.

The storm struck.

His staff snapped.

He screamed.

And it was gone.

The ranks broke. Some fled. Some begged. Some dissolved.

***

The Heartstone pulsed steadily. The crack a scar, not a wound.

The last feather fell.

Silence.

Not forgetting.

Remembrance.

The field lay quiet.

Smoke drifted from broken weapons.

Ash swirled like lost prayers.

Ríona stood, her mantle settling. The Heartstone pulsed not with alarm, but with mourning.

The Silent Warrior moved among the fallen. The crow sang no songs.

The land had been wounded. Old memory lines scorched.

The Hollowed had scattered.

Not destroyed. Not yet.

Ríona pressed her hand to the ground.

***

It trembled. Not in fear. In exhaustion.

The Silent Warrior brought her a spiral stone, its glyphs faint but breathing.

She knelt before it, fingers tracing old songs.

No tears.

Only vow.

Only path.

The crow rested beside her.

Wounded. Alive.

The land would heal. Partly.

But not completely.

She rose.

She was no longer guardian alone.

She was bearer.

A flame in a world that forgot it needed fire.

She turned westward.

Toward Newgrange.

The Silent Warrior followed.

The crow circled above.

Beneath a sky of bruised gold and fading mist, they left the field of crows behind.

(♪ Song: "Ash and Feather", see Appendix I)

The passage closed behind her, sealing her in breath and stone. No torches lit the way. No light pierced the dark. Only memory guided her.

194

She moved by touch and by the steady rhythm of the Heartstone, its warmth pressing against her chest.

The spiraled walls whispered as she passed. The chamber opened ahead, three recesses hollow of bone, waiting.

At its center, the altar waited.

She approached and, with slow reverence, placed the Heartstone upon the slab.

It pulsed.

The stone walls shimmered. The air thickened. The chamber stirred with presence.

The scent of rain on the soil and ironed blood rose.

Shadows shifted, not fearsome, but vast.

The Heartstone glowed, its fire threading into the altar like roots seeking the deep.

Ríona laid her hands upon it, not to summon, but to remember.

Songs rose in silence. Not sung, known. Of stone and seed, ash and river, crow and bone.

Her spirit braided memory into the broken world.

***

The earth answered: a low hum, a breath, and then, her name.

Ríona.

The light slowed. It lived.

She withdrew her hands.

The balance was not the old one restored, but a new weave. And her name was stitched within it.

She rose, heavy with all she had given, and what she had chosen to keep.

A crow called once.

Ríona turned.

She had restored what could be saved. She had buried what could not.

Now, she would carry both into whatever world awaited beyond the veil.

Buried what could not.

And now, she would carry both into whatever world awaited beyond the veil

CHAPTER 21

THE RESTORATION OF BALANCE

E very blade of grass, every stone half-buried in mist, every whisper of river air bent toward her passing.

Ríona moved through the ancient fields with the slow certainty of tide returning to a long-abandoned shore.

The Silent Warrior walked at her side, though his presence was as much shadow as substance now, a guardian, a witness.

Above, the crows circled high, silent and sparse, no longer the vast storm that had answered her call.

The Heartstone pulsed faintly against her chest, no longer burning but steady, a heartbeat braided with memory and promise.

***

Ahead, Brú na Bóinne rose from the earth like a buried giant's brow, its white quartz facade dulled by centuries of rain and sun, its grassy mound bowed under the weight of forgotten rites.

Yet it still stood.

Still waited.

The massive entrance stone lay untouched, its spirals worn thin by time, still whispering their truths to anyone who dared listen.

Ríona slowed as she approached, her fingers brushing the ancient glyphs. She felt the faint tremor of the old songs thrumming beneath the stone.

The Silent Warrior remained at a respectable distance, understanding what this place demanded.

She had left this ground as a priestess clothed in rites and expectations.

She returned now, not as one who served the gods, but as one who bore them.

The Heartstone throbbed gently, as if sensing the nearness of home, yet mourning the cost of its journey.

The crow perched up on a standing stone near the entrance, tilting its head, watching.

Waiting.

***

Ríona placed her palm flat against the cold surface of the entrance stone.

A ripple traveled outward, not of light, but of *memory*.

The air thickened.

The earth beneath her feet seemed to draw breath.

The stones remembered her.

The soil remembered her.

The hidden bones of ancient kin deep beneath the mound stirred in recognition.

Not just Ríona.

But all she now carried.

All she had become.

The passage into the mound opened easily without pushing or chanting.

As if the earth itself acknowledged the weight of her vow.

The sky above dimmed, clouds drawing tight over the horizon.

This was not a storm.

This was the closing of the veil.

A preparation for rite.

Ríona turned to the Silent Warrior.

He inclined his head once, placing a fist over his heart.

He would not follow.

The final steps must be hers alone.

***

The crow called once, a sound low and raw, a farewell wrapped in a blessing.

Without hesitation, Ríona entered the dark.

The earth swallowed her.

And the stones of Newgrange closed their breath around her steps.

(♪ Song: "The Crows Will Carry Me", see Appendix I)

The chamber held its breath.

For a long moment, Ríona believed it was finished, the Heartstone resting, the rite sealed.

But the earth had other designs.

The air thickened once more, not with mist, but with presence, a slow rising tide of weightless gravity felt not on the skin but in the marrow.

From the edges of darkness, from the spaces between the stones, from the memory woven into every grain of the mound's bones. The gods stirred, not as figures stepping forth in a grand parade or as voices booming from unseen heavens.

They awakened in subtler ways:

A flicker of gold dust where no light touched. The faint scent of wild honeysuckle and damp oak, thickening the air with old growth.

The low murmur of river water running beneath the stone, though no river flowed there.

Ríona stood still, hands at her sides, heart steady.

She did not kneel.

She did not speak.

This was not supplication.

This was communion.

***

She sensed them before her mind's eye, and deeper, in the woven fiber of her being.

The heavy and slow Dagda, the great cauldron of life, is trembling at the edge of renewal.

Danu, the river mother, is outstretched to cradle loss and hope.

Brigid, flame and forge, her loom clattering anew with the threads of broken and mended fate.

Lugh, bright warrior dimmed, yet nodding once, a glint of tempered steel in his unseen hand.

Aengus, bearer of dreams, watching with a sorrowful smile, love lingering in ruins and rebirth alike.

They did not speak.

They did not command.

They witnessed.

Ríona lowered her gaze, not in shame, but in understanding.

The gods had not abandoned the world.

The world had forgotten how to see them.

It was not their strength that waned, but the memory of their songs upon mortal lips.

She was not here to restore their former dominion.

She was here to remind the earth that it could remember, even if only in fragments, dreams, or whispered stories.

The Heartstone pulsed once beneath the altar, a slow, living thrum, and the presences faded, receding into the deep currents of stone and river and bone.

Not gone.

Sewn deeper.

Safe for a bit longer.

Ríona let out a slow breath.

***

The earth around her, the mound itself, settled as if exhaling after holding its lungs full for centuries.

She touched the altar one last time, a silent promise.

She would bear them forward, not as a priestess, queen, or thrall, but as flame, memory, or bridge.

A faint warmth brushed her cheek, like a mother's hand, a farewell, a beginning.

She turned toward the passage, the way open before her, and stepped into the waiting dark.

The passage breathed her out.

Cool air pressed against Ríona's face as she emerged from the heart of Brú na Bóinne, stepping once more into the living world.

The sky had shifted.

***

Not clear, not stormed, a tapestry of pale silver mist and faint gold, as if the earth hovered between waking and dreaming.

The Silent Warrior stood at the entrance, his blade sheathed, his hands folded across his chest in silent greeting.

The crow perched on his shoulder now, feathers slicked close to its body, its gaze sharp and solemn.

Ríona met their eyes and nodded once, not a command, not a farewell, but a bond renewed.

The stones around Newgrange hummed faintly underfoot; a vibration felt more than heard.

The rite was complete.

The Heartstone slept within the mound now, not as a weapon or a prize but as a seed.

A memory rooted in the body of the land itself.

It would not restore the world as it had been.

It would not undo the forgetting that had thinned the gods' presence.

But it would hold the thread intact, fragile, stubborn, enduring.

Ríona stepped forward, feeling the weight of her mantle settle heavier upon her shoulders.

The marks upon her skin still throbbed faintly, the spirals and runes now entirely woven into her flesh and spirit.

She was no longer simply the Morrígan's priestess.

She was her bearer.

Her voice when silence was needed.

Her blade when memory faltered.

The crow launched from the Silent Warrior's shoulder, soaring above them, a single figure cutting across the shifting sky.

Ríona lifted her gaze, following its arc.

There would be other battles.

Other veils to mend.

Other songs to sing or bury.

But this place, this moment, had been reclaimed.

Not perfectly.

Not completely.

But truly.

The Silent Warrior fell into step beside her without a word.

Together, they turned away from Newgrange.

They walked not back toward the villages, not back toward the places of men who crowned themselves in iron and forgetting.

They walked westward, toward the thin places, the broken paths, and the work that memory demanded.

***

And behind them, hidden beneath stone and mist, the Heartstone pulsed within the earth, a steady, stubborn breath, a reminder that memory, once carried, could never be entirely lost

CHAPTER 22

THE LAST GIFT

The path westward stretched before her, a thin line drawn across a landscape breathing with mist and memory. Ríona walked it alone.

The Silent Warrior had remained behind at the threshold of Newgrange, understanding without words that this part of her journey could not be shared.

The crow, too, had taken flight, vanishing into the mist like a whisper swallowed by the hills.

Only the faint, steady pulse of the Heartstone deep within the earth, distant now, no longer her burden to bear, marked the place she had left behind.

Each step pulled her farther from the world she had once known.

No village fires lit the horizon.

No songs drifted on the wind.

Only silence, vast, weighty, alive.

It was not the silence of absence.

It was the silence of transformation.

Ríona pressed a hand to the faint glyphs still warm upon her skin, feeling the steady thrum of the vow she had sealed within stone and spirit.

She had fulfilled her task.

And yet the weight did not lift.

If anything, it grew heavier with each breath, not a burden placed upon her by another, but a knowing carried deep within her bones:

She was no longer simply of the mortal world.

She was no longer returning to the world — she was becoming its echo. The part that remembered when all else forgot.

The thin places, the borderlands where memory and dream wove themselves into the soil, called to her now, threading her steps toward a future unseen by mortal eyes.

The mist thickened as she walked, swallowing the road, the hills, the edges of thought.

Time frayed.

She could no longer say if it was night or day, spring or autumn.

Only the slow cadence of her heart, only the whisper of the land remembering itself, guided her onward.

She walked with no map but memory, each footstep an echo of those who had come before.

The land did not speak, but it listened.

A grove appeared through the mist, a circle of ancient yews, their limbs twisted into cruel and kind shapes, roots gripping the earth as if cradling old secrets.

The air within the grove was still.

Expectant.

Ríona hesitated at its edge, her silence pressing heavier against her ribs.

She knew, without vision, without omen, that she was not alone.

The mist shifted beside her, not wind, not shape, but presence.

A pressure just behind her ribs, as if someone stood at her back, silent and still.

Ríona did not turn. She knew the Morrígan's gaze when she felt it, the weight of unspoken judgment wrapped in ancient memory.

There would be no voice. No command. Only presence. Only witnessing.

The last thread was drawing tight.

The last breath of her old self was ready to be exhaled.

She stepped into the circle.

And the world changed.

***

The grove breathed her in.

Ríona stood still within its heart, the mist clinging close, heavy with the scent of rain-soaked earth and old iron.

The yews arched overhead like the ribs of some ancient beast, their branches weaving a vault to hold the world's quiet.

And in the center of that stillness, She felt her. Not seen. Not heard. *Felt.*

The Morrígan did not descend with storm or scream.

She unfolded from the mist, a figure wrought from shadow and memory.

First, a woman, tall and cloaked, her hair a dark river crowned in twisted horn and feather.

Then a crow, wings half-furled, talons pressed against the yielding soil.

Then, a battlefield, banners fell, blood gleaming like spilled stars across shattered shields.

She was all of it.

She was the echo of what had been and the shape of what must endure.

Ríona did not kneel.

She bowed her head, a warrior's greeting, an equal's sorrow.

The Morrígan moved forward without footsteps, the earth not daring to groan beneath her.

Between them, no words passed.

There were none sufficient.

Only the long, slow breathing of the land.

Only the silent thunder of memory stirring.

The goddess raised one hand, not in command or blessing but in *recognition*.

In acknowledgment of what had been surrendered and forged, she stepped forward, not in defiance, but in remembrance.

Ríona lifted her gaze, meeting the eyes that were both crow and storm, woman and war.

No fear trembled in her.

Only the certainty of the path chosen.

The Morrígan stepped closer until the distance between them was only a breath.

She reached out, and with two fingers, traced a spiral over Ríona's heart, a mark deeper than flesh, unseen by mortal eyes, unerasable by time.

***

Ríona felt it bloom within her, a flame that did not burn, a silence that did not hollow, a song that needed no voice.

It was not a gift of power.

It was not a weapon.

It was *being*.

The final weaving of herself into the fabric of what would endure beyond the crumbling of stones and the silencing of songs.

The Morrígan's hand lingered only a moment longer, then withdrew.

The mist thickened between them.

The goddess's form blurred, not fading but folding back into the land, into the breath of crows and the heartbeat of rivers.

Until only the grove remained.

And Ríona.

Bearing the last gift not in her hands, but in her blood, in her breath, in her very being.

The spiral traced over her heart burned softly, not with pain, but with recognition.

Ríona pressed her hand against the unseen mark, feeling its slow, inexorable weaving into the marrow of her bones, the threads of her spirit.

The gift was not strength.

Not immortality.

It was *anchoring*.

Binding not to any single place but to the spaces *between*, between memory and forgetting, between life and death, between the mortal breath and the silence beyond it.

She was no longer tied to the ordinary wheel of life.

She would not wither with the seasons.

She would not die as mortals did.

But neither would she ascend among the gods.

She would endure, as memory, witness, and flame carried through the crumbling halls of fading songs.

Ríona looked down at her hands.

They trembled, not from fear, but from the sheer vastness of what she had become:

She would walk where the veil thinned, unseen by most, a whisper stitched into mist and crow call.

She would guard the fragile bridges between the world of men and the old places still pulsing beneath soil and stone.

She would kindle remembrance where it guttered low.

She would bury it where it became a blade too sharp for the living.

This was the last gift:

Not to rule.

Not to rest.

But to carry the weight no others remembered needed bearing.

She closed her eyes, breathing in the deep scent of the grove, earth and sap and the faint metallic tang of old blood.

The world had changed.

The gods had faded, not into death, but into distance.

The mortal world would move on, hungering for conquest, forgetting its roots.

And she would walk the spaces between.

Forever unseen.

Forever watching.

Forever remembering.

She did not weep.

There was no mourning in her.

Only acceptance.

Only slow, solemn peace.

The kind found in the heart of winter, beneath snow and stone, where life sleeps but does not die.

She opened her eyes.

The mist had thinned.

The path ahead waited, not back to villages or hearths but forward into the places where memory flickered like the last ember of a dying fire.

She would tend it.

She would carry it.

She would be its flame.

And through her, though none might know her name, the world would remember.

She walked on, not to be seen, but to keep the ember lit where silence once reigned.

The wind did not call her name.

But it carried her vow like breath across stone, into the long remembering of the land.

The mist curled at her heels, no longer binding or veiling.

It caressed her as she walked, not pushing, not pulling, but *welcoming*.

The grove fell away behind her.

Before her, the world unfolded in strange hues, deeper, older, as if her senses had slipped sideways into the marrow of the land itself.

She moved through fields where grass shimmered with forgotten names, past streams that sang low songs only she could hear, along stones that wept in silence, mourning prayers no longer offered.

Ríona's steps no longer pressed footprints into the earth.

Where she passed, the world stirred subtly, a crow lifting its head from a shadowed branch, a stream's surface rippling with unseen hands.

She was present.

And yet, already, she was becoming *other*.

Not fully mortal.

Not fully spirit.

A bridge.

A breath.

A flame against the cold hush of forgetting.

She crossed a low ridge crowned with thistle and hawthorn and paused.

Below her, in a small hollow, a woman tended a tiny fire.

A child sat at her side, head tilted upward, listening.

The woman spoke, not knowing the air carried her words farther than she intended.

She spoke of the old ways, of the Morrígan's crow, of a flame that walked the hills unseen.

Of a protector in the mists, who bore no crown and claimed no throne but who carried memory when all others forgot.

The child listened with wide, solemn eyes.

Ríona watched, unseen.

And in that moment, she understood:

She would not need temples.

She would not need songs carved in stone.

Memory would root itself wherever the land was loved, wherever stories were whispered beneath the open sky, wherever one hand reached for another in the dark and remembered.

***

She turned away from the ridge, her heart heavy and light.

The thin places waited.

The veil stretched thin across the western hills, the river valleys where the sídhe danced unseen, and the deep forests where dreams still touched waking life.

She would walk there, not as a savior, nor as a queen, but as a flame carried forward by those who would never know her name yet would feel her passing: a breath against their cheek, a crow's cry in the morning mist, a shiver at the edge of sleep when the old songs stirred.

Ríona stepped into the thinning mist.

And became the bridge the world did not know it was still needed.

CHAPTER 23

THE GUARDIAN OF THE VEIL

"When the mask cracks, it does not reveal the face.
It reveals the silence beneath it."
— Fragment from the Book of the Hollow Veil

T he seasons turned, but she did not.
Ríona moved through the waking world unseen, a ripple where mist gathered too thick, a shiver where the crow's call broke the hush before dawn.

She walked through the forests where the trees remembered their names in the old tongue.

She crossed rivers where stones still held the warmth of prayers whispered by long-vanished hands.

She stood at the edges of crumbling circles of stone, where once the gods had danced and mortal hearts had dared to dream beyond the veil.

None saw her.

Not truly.

Children sometimes glanced up from their games, frowning into the mist, sensing a presence they could not name.

Kneeling by hearths, old women would pause mid-prayer, feeling a blessing carried on the smoke.

Fishermen along black rivers would cross themselves unknowingly, whispering thanks to shadows they did not fear.

Ríona moved through it all, not as flesh, not as wraith, but as memory embodied.

The marks once etched into her skin had faded from mortal sight, but they burned steady beneath the surface of her being, guiding her steps along paths that few could tread and fewer could hold.

She did not sleep.

She did not hunger.

She existed in the in-between.

***

Where a boundary thinned, she was there.

Where a memory flickered, she wove herself through it, stitching the broken threads with patience, sorrow, and fierce, quiet love.

The veil between the worlds had grown ragged in places, torn by mortal forgetting, by the slow erosion of song and sacred soil.

But it had not fallen.

But it had not fallen, because she was there: tending, bearing, witnessing, not through grand battles, nor miracles carved across the skies, but through the slow, stubborn work of keeping the world breathing, unseen and undemanding.

She was not worshiped.

She was not praised.

She was not even remembered by name.

And she asked for nothing more.

The land carried her memory in the curve of rivers.

The crows stitched her stories into the winter wind.

The stones warmed themselves on her passing breath.

Ríona walked between.

212

And because she walked, the world still dreamed.

She did not guard the veil for praise.

She did it for the memory of names no one remembered, and the silence that still answered them.

***

There were places where the veil wore thinner than breath.

Sacred hills where grass grew in silent spirals.

Springs where the water ran too clear, too cold, and dreams clung to its surface like drifting leaves.

Caves that yawned beneath the earth, breathing mist scented with iron and unseen flowers.

Ríona knew each one.

She moved among them like a keeper tending a fragile fire.

At ancient wells, she brushed her fingers over stones etched by forgotten hands, whispering no words yet mending what memory could.

At ruined shrines swallowed by ivy and ash, she stood vigil until the wild things returned, fox, owl, and crow, claiming the places left hollow by human hands.

At river bends where the sídhe once gathered under starlight, she pressed her palms into the soil, feeling the ache of distance, of dwindling, and she sang silently into the rootwork.

The thin places were fraying.

Every year, the mortal world pulls harder away, away from breath shared with unseen things, wonder, and the terror and beauty of the in-between.

But where the veil wore too thin, where it tore, Ríona was there.

Mending with silence.

Weaving with presence.

Kindling memory with the warmth of her unseen passing.

Sometimes, those walking nearby would pause, feeling a brush against their shoulder, hearing a crow cry in a pattern that stirred ancient longings, seeing a shadow that did not frighten but steadied.

They did not know why, but they remembered, in the turning of a head toward the mist, in the clenching of a heart at the first winter frost, in the way a mother's lullaby carried the old melodies without knowing their source.

Memory stitched itself into the breath of the world through her.

Quiet.

Patient.

Unseen.

Ríona touched each thin place with care, not sealing them entirely, not cutting them away.

They were wounds, yes.

But they were also windows.

To seal them would be to kill what still lived.

To leave them untended would be to invite unraveling.

She tended them the only way she could, with balance, with love braided through sorrow.

And through her tending, the worlds did not drift entirely apart.

Not yet.

Not while she walked.

Though her feet left no mark upon the soil,

Ríona's passing carved deeper paths than stone.

***

In villages tucked along misted coasts, elders spoke of a spirit that lingered near the ancient wells, a shadow glimpsed when offerings of milk and bread were left on crumbling stones.

In the hills where the Mourning Trees grew thick, hunters told of hearing songs in the branches at twilight, no words, only the memory of a voice that once carried the names of the dead into safekeeping.

214

In the dark folds of deep forests, children who strayed too near the thin places would return with dreams of a woman crowned in black feathers, her hand outstretched, not to harm, but to guide.

None spoke her name.

Few even realized they remembered her.

But across the breath of generations, Ríona wove herself into the quiet spaces between words and wonder.

A crow is seen at a crossroads.

A sudden stillness before a storm.

A spiral is drawn absentmindedly into the dust by a child's hand.

In these small ways, she endured, not in temples of stone, nor in great songs sung by gathered choirs, but in the pulse beneath the river's skin, in the hush of mist settling over worn cairns, in the aching certainty deep within the human spirit that there was something worth remembering, even if the name was lost.

She had no need for shrines.

The land itself was her temple.

The breath of those who paused and *felt* was her prayer.

The trembling of the veil where dream and waking brushed was her hymn.

Ríona smiled sometimes, unseen, not in triumph, sorrow, or understanding.

Legacy was not measured by crowns or monuments.

It was measured in the moments when memory woke quietly inside a beating heart, asking nothing but to be carried forward, without fear, without claim, without forgetting.

Where the world thinned, she waited.

In the hush between midnight and dawn, frost silvered the fields, and every breath seemed to be borrowed.

In the sigh of rivers carving their silent songs into the earth's bones.

In the hollows beneath ancient stones, where moss and shadow clung together, names forgotten by mortals still sang in the soil.

Ríona stood, not as queen or saint, but as memory embodied.

At the broken edges where the veil fluttered loose, she watched and wove, gathering what fragments could be saved, bearing witness to what must be let go.

When a mortal heart, adrift in sorrow or longing, brushed too near the veil, she was there, guiding, steadying, sometimes sending a crow to cry once, sharp and accurate, to call them back.

When a child dreaming wild dreams stumbled into a thin place, she was the unseen hand steering them safely home.

When the ancient sites, the circles, the wells, the cairns, wept for lack of song, she stood in silence, stitching their sorrow into the breath of the land.

She asked for nothing.

She demanded no offering.

Her vigil was not for praise or remembrance.

It was for the balance, the breath held between forgetting and remembering, between fading and becoming.

The seasons spun their endless wheel.

Empires rose and crumbled.

Languages shifted like riverbeds drying and reforming.

But Ríona remained.

A shadow on a high ridge at sunset.

A whisper between stones where no path should run.

A crow perched at the edge of a sacred spring, watching with eyes too old for the briefness of human years.

She was the flame that did not consume.

The silence that did not abandon.

The bridge did not falter, even when the world forgot it was needed.

And so, she watched.

And so, she waited.

And so, she carried memory forward into every breath of mist, every spiral of frost, every dream that stirred a soul to wonder where no name remained.

Ríona, the flame of the Otherworld.

Ríona, keeper of the broken song.

Ríona, guardian of the veil

EPILOGUE

THE SILENT WATCHER

In time, the world forgot.

Rites faded from riverbanks and hollow hills. Cairns crumbled. Songs that once spun golden thread between breath and the unseen unraveled into lullabies whose meanings were long lost.

But some things endure beyond memory.

In the mist curling along forgotten paths, travelers sometimes felt a breath not their own, not with fear, but with the sense of being seen.

A crow on a fencepost before a storm, watching a place just beyond sight.

Children dreaming in river light glimpsed a woman crowned in feathers and flame, her eyes vast, sorrowful, endless. Her name was no longer spoken, but the land remembered.

The rivers whispered her passing. The stones still held the warmth of her vigil.

***

Ríona, who once knelt before the Heartstone with blood on her hands and stars in her hair, still walked.

Not as mortals count footsteps. Not as gods demand remembrance.

She bore the flame no others could.
She held the silence no others dared.

***

And through her, the old songs, broken and battered, endured.

Not yet lost.

But even legends fray.

Older things stirred beneath roots so deep even the sídhe turned their faces away.

Not shaped by mortal will.

Not softened by divine song.

Hollowed things, hungry and half-formed, pressed against the veil , thin now as a sigh.

They remembered too.

But not with love.

And though Ríona watched, though the flame held, the world's breath grew shallow.

The river of memory ran colder.

At the farthest edge of dreaming, something waited.

Something waking.

Not all things forgotten are harmless. And not all that stirs in silence seeks to heal.

And soon, even a silent watcher might be called to step from the mist, blade in hand, song in breath, to kindle the flame anew.

And yet, even memory, when left untended, begins to dim.

Seasons turned. Stones slumbered. Names unraveled from the tongues of children who no longer asked their meaning. The rites were spoken less often, the offerings given with uncertain hands. Across the veils, the gods waited, not in wrath, but in silence. Watching.

Far to the south, beneath a sky of ash and ashless fire, a girl stood alone in a hollowed grove where no birds sang. She heard a cry, not with her ears, but with something deeper, older.

A crow's cry. A flame's hush. A voice unspoken.

She did not yet know the name of Ríona.

But the mark burned beneath her skin, and the wind carried songs that had not been sung in an age.

And in the stillness between breaths, the world leaned in, not to remember, but to ask again: Who will carry the flame now?

But deep in the roots, where no name had ever been carved, something woke.

Not memory.

Not song.

Hunger.

APPENDIX I – SONGS OF THE CROWMOTHER

Ash and Feather

Sung by Ríona in farewell to the sacred grove of Brú na Bóinne.

Beneath the stones, the rivers sleep,
Names forgotten, vows to keep,
Nettled hands and thorn-wrapped skies,
Carry me where silence flies.

Threads unspooling in the mist,
Mother's voice and crow's last kiss,
Ash to ember, root to flame,
I walk the path that bears no name.

Feather falls, and flame endures,
Memory bleeds, but hope is pure,
I leave my voice upon the tide,
To find the dream the gods let die.

Thorn and sorrow guard the gate,
Time bends back and sings too late,
Oh, if I forget my face,
Let the nettles weave my place.

If you hear me through the veils,

Echoes of the Otherworld

> *In crow's lament or whispered trails,*
> *Bind my name to root and stone,*
> *And sing me back when I am gone.*

> *Feather falls, and flame endures,*
> *Memory fades, but vow is sure,*
> *I leave my voice upon the tide,*
> *And carry home the gods who cried.*

Lullaby of the Forgotten

Sung by Ríona to her mother in the tomb.

> *Sleep in the hollow where no names remain,*
> *Cradled by stone, untouched by flame.*
> *The wind remembers what none recall,*
> *Your song was silence, and silence was all.*

> *No thread was tied, no bell was rung,*
> *No crow had cried, no rite was sung.*
> *But still you drift in root and rain,*
> *A breath beneath the soil's refrain.*

> *Rest where the light forgets to fall,*
> *Rest where no footsteps come at all.*
> *Though none remain to speak your name,*
> *The lullaby still knows your flame.*

> *Sleep in the hush the gods once kept,*
> *Where even stars have knelt and wept.*
> *A shadow's grace, a mournful thread ,*
> *For those who sleep, and were not said.*

> *Rest where the light forgets to fall,*
> *Rest where no footsteps come at all.*

Though none remain to speak your name,
The lullaby still knows your flame.

Veilbound

Heard in trance by Ríona, the voice of the veil.

Beneath the skin, beneath the flame,
A thread remains without a name.
It pulls through breath, it pulls through bone,
It sings in silence, walks alone.

I do not sleep, I do not wake,
I am the vow the winds unmake.
I speak in dreams you dare not stay,
I turn the stars, I stain the day.

Veilbound, soul-spun,
Named by none.
Memory weeps where light has fled,
I call you back from what is dead.

I held your voice before your breath,
I'll hold it still beyond your death.
The ash forgets, the root obeys ,
You walk through fire, but do not blaze.

Veilbound, soul-spun,
Named by none.
If you return, return through me ,
The voice beneath the flame and tree.

Blood on the Threshold

Spoken at the crossing into the Otherworld.

Echoes of the Otherworld

> *I stood where stone and root divide,*
> *Cut my palm to choose the tide,*
> *One step more, the breath undone,*
> *The vow begins with what I've run.*
>
> *The earth did not call out my name,*
> *But still I walked, through ash and flame,*
> *No god did bless, no soul did wait,*
> *But I became the fire and gate.*
>
> *Blood on the threshold, dust in my tread,*
> *Memory silent, but never dead,*
> *I gave no prayer, I gave no plea,*
> *I gave the cost of being me.*

Wings Upon the Thread

A sacred solo sung in the voice of The Morrigan.

> *I watch from branch, from blade, from sky,*
> *Where threads are spun and kings will die.*
> *My wings are black, my breath is still,*
> *I do not judge, I only will.*
>
> *The wolf forgets, the crow does not,*
> *I name the wound the gods forgot.*
> *I walk in dreams you dare not keep,*
> *I guard the price of fire and sleep.*
>
> *Wings upon the thread,*
> *Song upon the dead,*
> *I speak the name you cannot flee ,*
> *And so the thread returns to me.*
>
> *I bind the blood, I mark the flame,*

I do not curse, I claim your name.
You offer vows with open palm,
I answer not with peace, but calm.

Wings upon the thread,
Song upon the dead,
I speak the name you cannot flee ,
And so the thread returns to me.

The root will rot, the stars will dim,
The blade will break before the hymn.
But I remain in ash and bone,
The crow that calls you not alone.

Wings upon the thread,
Song upon the dead,
I watch the path you dared to be ,
And now the thread returns to me.

Echoes of the Otherworld

The Tree of Fire

Sung by Ríona beneath the sacred tree.

> *The stars are falling, one by one,*
> *Ashes trailing from the sun,*
> *Their names are lost upon the wind,*
> *Forgotten where the light had been.*
>
> *A tree once burned at world's far edge,*
> *With roots of flame and sky for hedge,*
> *It sang in tongues no crow could speak,*
> *Its leaves were stars that dared to weep.*
>
> *And still it burns beyond the veil,*
> *Through shattered light, through mournful gale,*
> *The song remains though stars expire ,*
> *The prayer beneath the tree of fire.*
>
> *Its branches held the final breath,*
> *Of every vow, of every death,*
> *The dusk it sang was not the end,*
> *But fire returned, and stars to mend.*
>
> *I was born of ember's sigh,*
> *I will sing when stars all die,*
> *Let my voice be root and flame,*
> *Let the ash remember my name.*
>
> *And still it burns beyond the veil,*
> *Through shattered light, through mournful gale,*
> *The song remains though stars expire.*
>
> *The girl who sang beneath the fire.*

What the Flame Remembers

Heard in Ríona's transformation sequence.

I walked through fire and did not burn,
I sang the name the stars unlearned.
My skin is ash, my breath is thread,
I carry those the flame has fed.

The grove forgot, the river turned,
But still the blood beneath me yearned.
The stone was silent, but I heard ,
The echo of the unspoken word.

This is what the flame remembers:
Every vow that broke in embers,
Every hand that reached and fell,
Every name the shadows spell.

I rose where others could not stand,
I bore their silence in my hand.
The blade, the song, the stone, the sea ,
They all return through fire, to me.

This is what the flame remembers:
Not the wound, but how it trembles.
Not the fall, but how it rose.
Not the end, but what it knows.

The Crows Will Carry Me

Final song near Ríona's surrender.

When all is quiet, let me lie,
Beneath the breath, beneath the sky.
I gave my voice to fire and tree ,

Echoes of the Otherworld

Now let the crows remember me.

I sang of stars and broke the thread,
I walked with gods and called the dead.
But I will not return the same ,
The crow will cry, and call my name.

The crows will carry me, not far,
Just past the flame, just past the star.
Through shadowed bough and open sea,
The crows will carry what was me.

I do not ask for tomb or stone,
I do not need to walk alone.
The sky is black, the path is free ,
The crows have always flown for me.

The crows will carry me, not far,
Just past the flame, just past the star.
And where no memory dares to be,
The crows will carry me… through me.

APPENDIX II: PRONUNCIATIONS

(Note: These are approximations based on reconstructed Old Irish and Modern Irish pronunciation to help readers connect more deeply with the story's spirit.)

Word/Name	Pronunciation	Notes
Ríona	REE-uh-nuh	Means "queenly" or "regal."
Brú na Bóinne	Brew nah BOHN-yuh	"Palace of the Boyne", Newgrange.
Morrígan	MOR-ree-gahn	Goddess of war, fate, prophecy; "Great Queen" or "Phantom Queen."
Sídhe	SHEE	Fairy folk; spirits of the Otherworld.

Breasal	BRASS-uhl	Name meaning "strife" or "battle."
Fareth	FAH-reth	(Fictional) Druid name; rooted in Old Irish sound patterns.
Dagda	DAH-guh	Father-figure god; "the Good God."
Danu	DAH-noo	Mother goddess, associated with rivers and the earth.
Brigid	BRIH-jid or BREE-id	Goddess of poetry, healing, and smithcraft.
Lugh	LOO	Bright warrior-god; master of many skills.
Aengus	AENG-us	God of youth, love, and dreams.

Bóinne	BOHN-yuh	The Boyne River itself, sacred to the old traditions.
Otherworld	(Standard English)	The realm beyond mortal perception, where gods and spirits dwell.
Samhain	SAH-win or SOW-in	Festival marking the beginning of winter and the thinning of the veil.
Heartstone	(Standard English)	A sacred artifact within the story.
The Hollowed	(Standard English)	Spirits or beings that have lost memory and true form.
Crowstorm	(Standard English)	Mythic storm of crows summoned through Ríona's bond with the Morrígan.

APPENDIX III: HISTORICAL PLACES REFERENCED

(Some locations in this story are real sacred sites from Irish myth and history.)

Place	Description
Brú na Bóinne (Newgrange)	A prehistoric monument in County Meath, Ireland; older than Stonehenge and the pyramids. Built around 3200 BCE, sacred to the passage of the sun and spirits.
River Bóinne (Boyne River)	A river deeply woven into Irish mythology, associated with the goddess Bóinn and the site of many ancient battles and rituals.

Sídhe Mounds	Burial mounds and sacred sites believed to be entrances to the Otherworld, home of the fairy folk. Many dot the Irish landscape.
Hill of Tara (Teamhair)	The traditional seat of the High Kings of Ireland; a sacred place of kingship rituals and spiritual power.
Uaimh na gCat (Cave of the Cats)	A portal to the Otherworld located at Rathcroghan (Cruachan); associated with The Morrígan and Samhain legends.
Islands of the West	In legend, mystical islands beyond Ireland's shores, places where time stands still, spirits dwell, and mortal memory fades.

Author's Note

Echoes of the Otherworld began as a whisper, a story stirred from stone and shadow, rooted in the sacred silence of Brú na Bóinne. Though fictional, it is woven from the echoes of Ireland's mythic memory, shaped by the voices of women who walk the line between mortal and divine.

This book is a tribute to the power of land, ancestry, and story. The rites and ruins, the gods and spirits, are not relics of a forgotten past, they are living presences, felt beneath the skin of the world. I have taken great care to anchor the narrative in historical research, drawing from Iron Age Irish culture, authentic pre-Christian cosmology, and the deeper strata of oral tradition.

My creative lens is shaped by the enduring epic voice of Homer and the timeless theatrical rhythm of William Shakespeare. These influences echo throughout the cadence, structure, and spiritual tone of this book, in both the spoken lyric and the silences between.

Echoes of the Otherworld is the first novel published under my imprint, **Forgotten Rites Publishing**, founded to preserve mythic storytelling rooted in cultural authenticity.

Every word carries a prayer, to remember what was lost, to awaken what still lingers.

Thank you for walking the path with Ríona.

May the crows guide your steps.

— *Donald Quill*

Acknowledgments

Echoes of the Otherworld was shaped by many hands, seen and unseen. To those who supported this journey, your presence was the ground beneath each step.

To the ancestors of Ireland, whose stories ripple beneath stone, stream, and wind, this offering is made in reverence.

To the scholars, historians, and folklorists whose work helped light the ancient paths, your dedication made it possible to walk them anew. Deepest thanks to Lora O'Brien and Morgan Daimler, whose writings have been invaluable in grounding this tale in cultural authenticity.

To my earliest readers and supporters: Eddi Ashy, Carri Adams-Quill, Jen Mayes, Karen Klotz, Karen Swoffer, and Brandy Boyden McNiss, thank you for your careful eyes, your honesty, and your belief in this story before it had a spine to stand on.

To my readers, may this tale echo within you long after the final page.

— *Donald Quill*

About the Author

Donald Quill is a mythic fiction author whose work evokes the deep currents of ancestral memory, sacred landscapes, and the thin places between worlds. His stories are woven from the echoes of ancient cosmologies and grounded in meticulous historical research.

He is the author of *From the Threads of Silence*, a speculative exploration of memory, resistance, and inner voice, and *Echoes of the Otherworld*, the first novel released under his imprint, **Forgotten Rites Publishing**, founded to uphold mythic storytelling rooted in cultural authenticity.

When not writing, Donald studies pre-Christian Irish traditions, walks beneath crow-haunted skies, and listens for the whispers between wind and stone.

Preview of Book Two *The Stone That Would Not Cry*
Book Two of the Songs of the Crowmother

Seven years after the flames of prophecy reshaped Brú na Bóinne, the land grows restless again.

Neassa now bears the mantle of High Priestess, but peace proves fragile beneath omens, silence, and blood-soaked soil. A girl vanishes. A raven watches. And whispers rise of a stone that will not break, will not bleed, and will not weep.

In the east, rival tribes in Leinster gather for a reckoning, their blades sharpened not only for war, but for power over the memory of the gods.

And from the edge of the Otherworld, where mist remembers what mortals forget... Ríona hears the land's cry once more.

The Morrígan is not done. And neither is her chosen.

www.ingramcontent.com/pod-product-compliance
Lightning Source LLC
Chambersburg PA
CBHW050307110726
47899CB00007B/2146